RAPTURE REDUX

RAPTURE REDUX

By

Lindsey Martin-Bowen

Paladin Contemporaries * Scottsdale * Kansas City, Missouri

For information and permission, contact

Paladin Contemporaries
6117 E. Nisbet Road
Scottsdale, AZ 85254

Library of Congress Cataloging-in-Publication Data

Martin-Bowen, Lindsey.
Rapture Redux: a novel / Lindsey Martin-Bowen. First edition.

ISBN-13 978-1-881048-08-4
ISBN 1-881048-08-X
        1.   Fiction. 2. Comedy. 3. Mixed genres. 3. Science fiction.
        4. Social commentary. 5. Private eye.

Paladin Contemporaries, Scottsdale, Arizona. Kansas City, Missouri.

For my family—

*not only Carl, Aaron, Ki, Tim, Rook, and Ashe, but Rick (and Sandra),
Terry (and Jill), Andy (and Debbie), Clint (and Sheryle), Kathy (and
George) and Becky (and Jeff), and their children: Shawn, Kate, and
Karla; Valerie, Gerry, and Danny; Michael, Stephanie, and Colleen;
Nicole, Dustin, and Monica; Drew, Carter, and Tyler; and Luke, Jacob,
Brian, Michael, and Sarah, plus all of their spouses and children.*

Acknowledgments

Thank you to C.S. Lewis, whose brilliant novels and essays have influenced this novel.

Also thanks to the University of Missouri English Department's Creative Writing Program, I was able to embark upon a fiction-writing career in 1986 under the wise mentor, Dr. James C. McKinley, a renowned fiction writer. I appreciate all he has taught about writing fiction—and how to read fiction as a writer.

Rapture Redux is the sequel to *Cicada Grove*, the novella I wrote then. In 1987, the *Cicada Grove* manuscript won the Grand Prize in the Barbara Storck Creative Writing Contest, and its first chapter placed second in the Fiction category.

Also thanks to Chris Baty and other NaNoWriMo crew members who also made writing this novel possible.

PREQUEL
Snatched

New York City: August 10, 2015

Chelsey twisted one of her auburn ringlets and glanced around again for Michael. He should have been here by now. She'd waited thirty minutes, and she couldn't leave without him. She needed his help with the kidnapping case. And she wasn't sure if she'd recognize him. Mainly, she knew him from photos and his voice—a rushed Brooklyn accent. But she'd always heard his voice over the phone, often muffled by either the traffic outside or by her cell phone's static. It seemed she rarely got a clean connection—at least, not when it mattered. And she'd stuffed her android into the large Pullman she now dragged through La Guardia. No matter how hard she tried, she didn't like the smart phone. She couldn't scroll smoothly with her fingers and all too often, her coordination was off: She'd lose an Internet connection when her fingers fumbled on the tiny keypad. It irked her that both of her careers forced her to rely so much on technology, especially today.

She hit the speed dial for Jack, *The Globe*'s editor. No answer. She left a message: "Michael isn't at the gate. Help!"

Suddenly, from about three feet away, a bearded man in a white tunic and sandals interrupted her thoughts. His voice wailed like a shofar, its tone swelling then ebbing into a low moan. He chanted in a language she couldn't understand, perhaps Hebrew—or maybe Arabic. A narrow scar cut across the holy man's brow, but he seemed as oblivious of his appearance as he did the passersby bustling around him. The man's wails made her feel even more alone. He scared her so much, she scurried down the airport. Along the way, she inhaled whiffs of stale coffee that sent her stomach churning. Already, the stress over the missing model had made her system too acidic. She didn't need that pain, too. She hadn't looked forward to coming to New York. It was the second time she'd been to the Apple, and today, myriads of persons in motley attire—red dungarees to gray pin stripes—surrounded her. Their faces seemed to press against her, their noses enlarging as if she viewed them through a fish-eye lens.

She panted while she towed the Pullman and squinted at each face, unable to find the right one, the face in the snapshot she clutched. In it, a curly-haired Michael glowed with an open, toothy smile. A flirtatious grin. At first glance, his eyes seemed to glitter, but a darkness— dullness, really—emanated from his pupils, turning them into flat, black discs. Even if his charcoal suit and smooth, black eyebrows seemed sophisticated, and even if Chelsey found his face attractive, she still feared the man in the photo. Something about his deep-set, flat eyes made her feel uneasy. Even worse, now she couldn't find those eyes—eyes that frightened her—anywhere. Michael had agreed to meet her at the airport by three, but Chelsey's watch didn't show the correct time. She'd set it between ten and twelve minutes ahead because she didn't want to know the exact time when she rushed to interviews. This mode of operation ensured she'd arrive early. Besides, she preferred to see busy people when coming or going. That way, she could catch them off guard. But not today. She needed time to be exact. She pulled out her cell phone again and smirked. Giving the accurate time was the phone's sole reliable feature. It was 3:33 PM. This didn't help her nerves.

Although she was nervous about meeting Michael, she wasn't sure why. She wore a gray silk, skirted-suit because she wanted to make a good impression—show him that she was a grownup, a serious journalist, not some cub reporter working as a stringer. She didn't want him to know about her other profession. He might laugh. Besides, her work as a private eye was still a secret. Often she wore disguises *á la* Sherlock Holmes for that work. Today, she didn't dress like the fashion models that surrounded Michael, and she wondered if she should have. Instead of spiked or wedged heels, she wore pumps—even they slowed her down. She moved more quickly in sandals or boots. Plus, her panty hose kept slipping—forcing her to perform the usual shifting-the-crotch maneuver. It seemed more often than not, the waist bands gave on those nylon tyrants, so the crotch kept edging downwards toward her knees, and she'd have to take short, quick steps, moving like a Geisha across La Guardia's slick floor. She felt like a character in *The Mikado*.

"Chelsey McKay," the airport intercom blared. "Chelsey McKay to the United counter." Chelsey jumped. Surely that would be Michael waiting for her there. She whipped her Pullman around and headed toward the United desk. It was on the opposite end of the airport.

She'd only seen Michael in-person from a distance in at a runway show. Then, she'd focused on getting the best angles of the models and the spring collections with loose, gauzy skirts. And she'd been so rushed, she hadn't paid the keen attention to details the way she would normally. She remembered only Michael's peculiar limp and his gray-streaked hair, heavy eyebrows, and wide grin. And those eyes: pale green—or maybe blue. The fluorescent lighting had interfered with identifying eye color, but she remembered his eyes were an unusual color for a Jewish man. And today, she'd spotted no one with eyes similar to his. Even if several men strove through the airport with Michael's hurried gait, none matched his peculiar walk favoring the left hip, either. She had to find him soon. Staring at passengers disembarking, she scanned every face, each set of eyes especially. One man with curly, black hair and an eager grin caught her attention. "Michael?" she called, her voice breathy. She pressed her fingers together, digging her nails deeper into her camera bag strap, and she felt her shoulders tighten and a pain creep up her spine. The man didn't respond. Instead, he stared above the crown of Chelsey's head as if she didn't exist. Then, a blonde woman stepped out of the unloading tunnel, and the man lunged toward that woman. Chelsey sighed, scanned the room, and started hiking again.

Suddenly, from nowhere, a fly buzzed around her right shoulder. She leaned her head and torso back, but with both hands on straps—one gripping the camera bag, the other, her purse, she couldn't swat at the tiny beast. It flew higher for a second then charged smack-dab for the bridge of her nose. She stepped back, clutched the purse strap, and swung her purse in front of her face to scare the insect. She sent the purse in a wild arc, and the motion threw her off-balance. She wobbled and fell onto the floor. At least, the fly darted after another victim. Chelsey sighed.

Today, she wished she hadn't agreed to meet Michael at the airport. But she had to let him call the shots. Michael Levine was the one person close to Isadora Winger, the "Granite Goddess," a *Vogue* model who'd disappeared two weeks before.

"Talk with him," her editor Jack had sputtered then struck a match on his zipper and lit his pipe. "Get close. Grill him. Get the story. I've got faith in you." Today, she wasn't sure she had such faith in herself. She sighed again, stood, readjusted the camera strap over her left shoulder and tugged her Pullman to a bench nearby. She had to pull her mind back to earth before she rolled into United's counter. Surely it was

Michael who'd ordered her paged. He had to be at the gate. But the intercom didn't give his name. Forty minutes now of staring into strangers' eyes had started to wear on her, so she leaned back onto the bench and slipped the snapshot into a blazer pocket.

She also worried because she needed to pick up her Scout with the rest of her baggage. A miniature Doberman, Scout tended to be hyper, and she wasn't sure how long the sedative would calm him. The past two weeks, she'd lost her ability to soothe the dog, too. Indeed, the model's disappearance had unnerved her that much. Her knees had quivered when she'd phoned Isadora's brothers, sisters, aunts, uncles, former lovers, other models, and managers, each of them yielding conflicting clues to the fashion plate's whereabouts.

A former lover speculated that Isadora had "taken off for the Caymans," while a sister was sure she'd "hitchhiked to Colorado." And yet another sister swore the Granite Goddess had "grabbed an Atlantic flight to the British Isles." Then Michael Levine from *Women's Wear* had phoned Jack, his colleague from college newspaper days. Jack had whispered to Chelsey that Michael confided he was "onto something big" and claimed he could "find Isadora." Michael had also asked Jack to send him his "top investigator—one who isn't a wuss." And Jack had chosen her. She sighed again. *Surely, Michael must wait at the counter,* she thought. *That is, if he's still alive.* For once, she didn't felt good about being Jack's "Golden Girl." She'd taken *The Globe* position four years ago—not long after college, when she'd first gone undercover as a police detective. Then, she'd liked writing for a living so much, she'd decided to continue being a reporter. She quit the police department but continued working as a private eye—taking jobs here and there—so she enjoyed the best of both worlds, one public, one very private. Only Jack and her former guardian Neil knew of her dual career, and with her reporting job, the cases they referred to her were enough to fill her schedule. Later, Jack admitted he was glad he'd let her live that double life after she'd made a splash for the small daily by uncovering illegal contracts the city government had signed with foreign businessmen and with her story about election tampering.

Yet Isadora's story rattled Chelsey even more than those had. Questions about the missing model kept Chelsey awake till three a.m. almost daily. Then, after drifting off and thrashing through nightmares she couldn't remember—*she never could*—she'd awake sweating. She wondered if the model had been abducted by human traffickers—or perhaps drug lords. The model had a history with cocaine. Still Chelsey was so distraught, she'd phoned Neil, who'd raised her since she was three. After he'd asked her to come by and talk, he diagnosed her anxiety as "a subliminal, delayed reaction" to her mother's death. "You don't remember it," he'd said and leaned back in a recliner. He wrinkled his nose and twitched his lips. "But there was quite a stir the first day your mom didn't show at the office." He stroked his chin. "And police dicks and reporters hounded us so much the next week, we all wanted to take off for Bermuda to get away from everything—including our thoughts. So Isadora's disappearance is unearthing your unconscious memories. That's why it's affecting your sleep patterns. That's why you can't maintain the aesthetic distance you do with your other cases."

She considered he might be right. But his explanation quelled neither her churning stomach nor the nightmares. And it didn't abate the nausea that overcame her whenever she thought about the story. Especially today, it obsessed her when she thought about the holy man and tried to identify his unusual odor—was it myrrh? She rose from the bench to continue to the United counter.

Then, appearing from nowhere as much as the fly, a man in a black fedora marched toward her. Wrapped in a gray trench coat that hit him mid-calf, he squinted and scowled as he crossed the landing. The fedora shadowed his face so she couldn't see it well. Was it Michael? Had Michael grown a beard? But she could see the man's heavy eyebrows almost covered his forehead. He was plumper than she'd remembered Michael, and his face looked far darker.

About ten feet away, the man stopped abruptly, and he lifted then rotated his head in a manner that reminded Chelsey of a bulldog she had once owned. He scanned the crowd, then glared at Chelsey, and his eyes formed tight triangles. "You Chelsey McKay?" he barked in a gravelly voice as thick as his eyebrows.

She stared at him, squinted, and slid her right hand over her left, which held the suitcase handle. Then she released it and crossed her arms.

"Yes. Why? Are you—"

"Come with me," he barked. Before she could dodge his reach, he grabbed her arm and resumed marching at his incessant pace. Chelsey clutched her purse and tried to keep her camera bag from swinging. With the panty hose still moving southward, she couldn't keep up with him. She wanted to scream, but her throat felt dry, as if it were filled with fur. She felt she'd choke, and all she could manage was, "Why are you doing this? Who are you?" She panted. "Are you Michael?"

The man shook his head. Hair inside his nose wasn't trimmed, and his mustache curled over his upper lip and into his teeth, which were unusually yellow. He smelled of Jade East mixed with Musk. Chelsey speculated some shop had mixed the cologne for him. But she was certain this man couldn't be a regular employee with *Women's Wear*. She wondered if the magazine had hired the thug to escort her. If so, Michael wasn't much concerned about her comfort. This guy moved too fast and his grip hurt her arm. She tried pulling away from him, but he would not loosen his grip. She wasn't strong enough to make him. "Wait a minute—who are you?" she finally spat out. "Let me go or I'll scream!"

"Don't you need to meet somebody?" He dropped her arm.

"Yes." She rubbed the spot his fingers had gripped. "I need to pick up my dog."

"Dog?" His black eyes bulged like mushroom caps. "You brought a dog on a business trip?"

"I bring him everywhere." She crossed her arms.

"What kind of dog?" He squinted.

"Uh . . . a . . . mix." She bit her lip. Again she rubbed the arm he'd squeezed. "He's small." She hoped he wouldn't recognize Scout's breed. "I must get him. I simply must. And besides, who are you? I thought Michael was meeting me."

"He sent me." The man grimaced, and his gaze darted around the airport. He lowered his voice. "For protection."

"How do I know Michael sent you? Where are your credentials?"

"My what?" His Mideastern accent was more pronounced. He scowled again.

"IDs. Something with your name on it. Something that shows me you're taking me to Michael. And what's Michael's last name?"
"Levine." The man sneered and inhaled deeply, slid his right hand to his hip and patted it. The folds of his overcoat outlined a cameo of a pistol's handle. He grinned. "This is my—what you say? Credential? And you want to know my name? You can call me Ishmael."

Chelsey sighed and shook her head. "I must get my dog." She tugged her pantyhose as discretely as she could.

Fortunately, Scout still slept inside the pet carrier. After Chelsey had picked him up, then her other bags, Ishmael steered her down one corridor then another, then outside to a passenger pickup area where a charcoal limousine idled. Like Ishmael, the driver looked Mideastern. He chewed on a cigarette and flinched when he spotted Ishmael and Chelsey approaching the car. He was a small-built man whose large nose and lined face made him look like a weasel when he nodded. Ishmael pulled Chelsey toward the car, and the driver sprang out of it and opened the back door wide. "Good afternoon, Madame." His accent matched Ishmael's.

Chelsey nodded but said nothing. It seemed odd that Michael had hired these two Mideasterners who looked more like Arabs than Jews. That is, if he had hired them. Yet, the thought that they might be kidnapping her was too melodramatic—too bizarre. It was more than her mid-western mind could conceive. Something strange was going on, but it couldn't be that strange, surely. On the other hand, this man had just bullied her with his gun. She chided herself for not noticing that bulge in his pocket before he forced her to accompany him. She sighed again and glanced at Ishmael. "Where are we going?"

"Into the limousine." He frowned, and with a snarky tone that was almost a snarl, he clipped his words. After they slid inside and she positioned the pet carrier, Ishmael pressed a button that shot a partition across the window separating the front and back seats. It simultaneously drew curtains across all the other windows. Chelsey twisted a diamond and sapphire ring—an heirloom from her mother—and stared at her knees. She hoped they wouldn't start quivering. Ishmael pressed another button, and a small wet-bar unfolded from the wall below the partition. Chelsey looked up. He peeled the foil from the top of a bottle of *Sauvignon Blanc*, fiddled with the cork, and finally, poured two glasses. "Relax." He grinned sardonically again. Have some wine. Settle your nerves."

Chelsey frowned. She started to refuse, but then, she'd seen him break the seal. She sighed. "Maybe a little."

When she held the almond-colored wine to her nose, she picked up an unusual scent—something acrid like nail polish remover. She sipped it. It tasted like a *Sauvignon*. She sipped a bit more then drank a couple of large swallows.

"You like it?" Ishmael sipped from his glass then set it on the table. He pressed another button and her seat reclined. "Take it easy for a while. This is a long ride—maybe two hours. You might want to nap. So let your mind go. Relax . . . relax." Soothing, hypnotic now, his voice began to lull her to sleep. Still, she was determined to fight that enticement to nap. Suddenly, the car grew far too warm. She sipped the wine again. *Yes, it tasted fine, but did it smell as it should? Was something strange about the smell?* She sniffed it again. *No. It smelled fine.* Then, the car grew even warmer. She felt her muscles relax. Indeed they relaxed against her will. She didn't want to drop off to sleep beside this strange, foreboding man. And yet, she grew drowsy, and the drowsiness made her lose control. The car grew warmer yet—and stuffy. "Can we open a window?"

Ishmael pressed still another button, and a small wind shimmered behind the curtains on her right. Nonetheless, she felt fatigued—so fatigued—and her mind simply stopped. She closed her eyes and felt peace. All the nervous fury, all the tension of the past two weeks, simply lifted. It seemed ironic, that here in this car with this stranger—indeed, an odd stranger, she felt relaxed. Too relaxed.

CHAPTER 1
Message to Michael

Chelsey blinked. She smelled sandalwood incense and heard loud guitars and screeching voices. Around her, a group of youths—maybe as young as eighteen—dressed in black were dancing to heavy metal music. Jerking and twisting their bodies to blinking strobe lights, each of them wore glittered purple and blue eye shadow, scarlet rouge and ruby lipstick—males and females both. She couldn't name any of the dancers, yet they seemed oddly familiar, as if she'd been around them for years—as if she'd worked with them, gone to school with them, seen them each day of her life. But she couldn't name one specific face.

"Get up, woman!" a man called to her. He was one of the older ones—maybe in his upper twenties. "Dance!" The dark shadow over his eyes merged into wide, black, painted eyebrows. His teeth glowed like iridescent glass. She said nothing but pulled herself up and stared around the room. Splats of red and yellow paint were sprinkled across black walls, and gold paint dripped from pentagrams that someone had painted in each corner. Through a window, neon signs flashed "Joe's Bar and Grill" and street sounds of feet hitting pavement with the groan of traffic below made her sense she was still in the Apple—but she was not sure. It also seemed as if this could have been any dive in the dark quarters of almost any city in the states or in Western Europe.

"Babe, get with it!" The man with black eyebrows shouted now. She wobbled up, dragged her feet across the room, and wandered into a kitchen where more dancers jerked to loud music. Spaghetti sauce stained the walls, and here and there, clumps of vermicelli clung to them. A yellow, brackish film covered not only the walls, but the refrigerator, stove, and ruffled curtains, now faded from what looked as if it had once been a cheery peach color. She glanced at the antique blender and mixer, and just as she moved toward a coffee machine, she glimpsed a man resembling Michael Levine in another room—a parlor or library. She turned and stepped toward him, but the heavy black-eye-browed man had followed her into the kitchen. Now he grabbed her arm and shouted something unintelligible to the other dancers. All of them surrounded Chelsey, grabbed her, and pulled her to the floor. One of them still held her arm and shoved her into a corner. Then, she saw light reflect off the point of a steel needle as he slipped it under her skin.

After the drug's warm glow subsided, she blinked again, then turned her head away from the naked light bulb above. It hurt her eyes. When she lifted an arm to cover her face, she gasped. Pentagrams, fork-toothed candelabras, and letters that looked like Greek or Hebrew script had been tattooed on her left arm. She lifted her right one—someone had tattooed it with the same designs. She scurried to her feet. For some reason, the dancers now ignored her—and she could no longer see the man with the thick eyebrows. Still, the stereo blared cacophonous sounds, and dancers stretched and jerked in the kitchen. She slipped into the room where she'd seen Michael—or a man who appeared to be Michael—before she'd been attacked.

"Michael?" She called in a shaky voice. "Michael?" She wandered through the room. Another disc played there, but its sounds were quieter. It warbled, "Strawberry Fields Forever," a Beatles tune popular forty-five years before.

The youths sat in circles around the system and passed a pipe. They, too, wore vivid makeup, but they didn't dress in black. Instead, they wore paisley scarves, striped ponchos, jeans, and long, denim skirts. None of them seemed to notice Chelsey. They sat with eyes closed or eyes glazed over; some of them stared into space. "Michael?" she called again. A long-haired woman turned toward her. It stunned Chelsey because she'd often pictured herself looking like the woman who sat cross-legged by the entertainment system, long hair flowing, hoop earrings, a paisley peasant blouse with puffy sleeves, and a woven serape over her shoulders. It was an image Chelsey had once wanted to live but opted not to. In that world, she'd grow her own herbs, eat only whole grains, beans, and vegetables, and fill her kitchen with smells of curry and garlic. She'd till and plant a garden and write at least two poems every day. She'd no longer pry into lives to unearth lurid secrets hidden in the city's catacombs, no longer chase stories in the fast-paced world that now squeezed her life into a rectangular box. She sighed. That act wasn't happening, so she returned to her search for Michael.

She spotted a door in a corner. It looked as if it led to a bathroom. She opened it and stepped inside. The room was indeed a bathroom, tiled with mirrors. She stared into the mirror to examine her arms again. Under fluorescent lights, the markings were red, black, and blue, not the purple, muddy color she'd perceived before. Oddly, her arms weren't sore. Perhaps the witches and warlocks had merely inked-in tattoos with a hectograph. She tugged a wash cloth from a rack, rubbed in soap, and tried to scrub off a pentagram. The ink wouldn't budge. Her skin reddened, so she quit. She stared into the mirror again, drew back her bangs, and observed a small pimple that had ached for two days. It'd finally come to a head. She ran a forefinger over it.

"Sex cures those," Jake, a former boyfriend, had once told her. He'd had ulterior motives, she was sure. So she'd resigned herself to putting up with a few bumps on her skin rather than suffering the foibles of heartbreak. And sexual relationships without commitments were heartbreaks, she knew. When she was a small child, she saw her mother give love to men who merely used her. She saw her mother's self-esteem plummet so low, and the rest of the world—the business and publishing worlds—had used her, too. She saw her mother cry every night, over some man, over the lack of money, or because the men who ran newspapers and ad agencies kept her working late hours at the office or working weekends and evenings at home over light tables and paste-up boards. Chelsey would sit at her table, drawing and constantly looking toward her mother. And her mother would periodically glance up and force a smile. But it was the tired look in her eyes that still penetrated Chelsey's memories. She'd watched her mother slave over paste-up boards late at night. Chelsey had been so young, she vaguely remembered her mother's series of relationships. But later, after Chelsey had entered puberty, Neil filled in the details. So if empty sex meant a clear skin, she preferred the pimples.

She popped this one, dabbed her forehead, and slipped back into the main room where the Hippie-like youths sat. She watched them pass a bong and shook her head. Michael must know this was happening here—yet he went along with it. Perhaps these kids worked for him. She scanned the room. Surely he wouldn't have left. The room had changed, too. Somehow it had morphed into the front room with the black walls, pentagrams, and bright colors now swirling like shards in a kaleidoscope. "Michael," she called again, her voice wavering. "Michael?" She was thankful the dancers now ignored her. "Michael? Michael!" she repeated then realized she was screaming. "Michael! Michael." The colors on the wall grew more brilliant, and the disc wailed louder. But no one answered. She still groaned Michael's name while she thrashed in her seat and awoke, sweating. She blinked at the bright light filtering through a plane window. She looked at her arms. There were no tattoos, no signs of any markings. Next to her, Ishmael sat with his head back against the seat as if he were dozing. He clutched a .45 resting in his lap. She tapped his shoulder. "Where are we?"

He blinked, leaned forward, and grinned. "You wanted to meet Michael Levine.

"Yes. But I didn't need to fly again to see him. He's in New York. What's going on?" She raised up in the seat and crossed her arms.

Ishmael turned away and nodded across the aisle. "There's Mr. Levine."

The man on the other side had thinner cheeks than the man in the photo, and the gray streaks now fanned out from his temples and covered most of his head. But yes, it was Michael Levine in a gray pinstripe sitting there and reading a magazine. He glanced up, and Chelsey opened her mouth to call to him but stopped when she spotted a handcuff on one of his wrists. It locked him to the seat. She stared at him a second longer then swung back to Ishmael.

"What's happening here? Where are we going?"

Ishmael grinned, showing his yellow teeth. "Lebanon."

Her throat felt furry again. Even if reporting and hunting for clues thrilled her, she feared covering the Mideast. The 9-11 Twin Towers disaster had rattled her. With Ishmael's words, her arms stiffened, and her chest tightened. She felt pains over her sternum yet she managed to cough out, "But why?" She shook her head and tried to hold back tears. Even if her hopes about the trip had been dashed, she didn't cry.

"You're needed there." He frowned. Still clutching the pistol, he crossed his arms, and his black fedora slid over his forehead. She wished he'd drop the gun.

"What about my dog?"

He didn't look up. "In the baggage compartment."

"What? I want him here."

Ishmael frowned. "There's air back there. He'll be fine."

Chelsey crossed her arms. She hoped Scout would pee on the floor—and she hoped his smelly pee would spread through the baggage compartment of this private jet. But then, it'd smell up the carrier, too. She also worried about her possessions. "And my camera?"

Ishmael lifted his fedora and glared. "You won't need it."

"Who are you to say?" She started to stand but the seat belt reigned her in. "Look, you bully. That's my camera. It's a Nikon. It's an antique, and I can't afford to replace it. I need it."

"You think we are fools?"

"I don't care if you confiscate my film. Throw it away. But that camera's been in my family for a generation. It's mine—"

Ishmael blinked. Then slowly, he grinned. "Okay. You'll get your camera when we land. But I am keeping the film. The prince will like to see it. He must investigate to see if your company's been spying on him or his enterprises. He will discover why you have come here. And until he discovers your mission, you will be under my guardianship."

What prince? she wondered. She sighed, leaned back on the seat, and looked out the tiny window at clouds roiling into shapes like camels following one another in a hazy caravan. She lifted a forefinger to her mouth and chewed on a cuticle, then tried again to re-position the pantyhose. Now she would have to use one of the phones to shoot photos. Even if she could transmit them instantly, she couldn't create the artistic shots the Nikon produced. She sighed and shifted her weight from hip to hip. And still, the pantyhose continued to slide down her thighs. It hadn't turned out to be a good day.

CHAPTER 2
Attic Dreams

When Chelsey returned to sleep, she dreamt she was in an attic, where she coiled inside an old cardboard box. The musty air filled her with a strange sensation—as if she were living in a fairy tale, Hansel and Gretel or Red Riding Hood—one of those stories set in dark, hidden woods. She awoke in her dream, climbed outside the box, and explored the dark room where spiders had built condominiums in corners, and stacks of notebooks, files, and old trunks collected dust. She ran a forefinger across an old upright, steamer truck. The dust spun in the air and irritated her nose. She sneezed.

Then she found an old, brown leather album with peeling gold letters. She opened it and ran her fingers across the slick sheets covering photos mounted with the tiny corner triangles on black felt-textured pages. The album contained snapshots of her mother. Chelsey flipped through it and discovered photos she'd never seen—early studio photos and snapshots of her mother and father together. They looked happy, mostly, except for the wistful expression in her mother's eyes. Chelsey stared at the photos, and especially at her mother's face a few minutes, then she slammed the cover shut. She leaned back, squinted, and stared at the ceiling. She couldn't shake the image of her mother's expression—sad, so empty. Chelsey closed her eyes. Her mother's eyes floated before her. Then they multiplied and morphs into thousands of sets of eyes forming a strange kaleidoscope, each of the eyes retaining the patterns of that haunting, sad expression. The eyes stared at Chelsey, even after she opened her eyes. In her dream, the eyes still stared at her from the walls throughout the night. Like stars or planets, the eyes glimmered and pulsed with green lights.

In fact, when Chelsey awoke, she blinked and stared at the wall, which retained a ghost of the blinking eyes she'd seen in her dream. She stared at the wall a long time before she thought about the strange case of Isadora and her own peculiar situation, which had grown odder every hour. She looked out the window again at the clouds, which had become dark clusters. She was determined to figure out what was going on.

First, Ishmael had abducted her from the airport. How could he spot her so quickly? Who had sent him? Obviously, not Michael Levine. How did the person who sent Ishmael know she would land there? No one outside of *The Globe* employees and Michael Levine knew she was arriving there today. In fact, unless there was a leak at *The Globe* or *Women's Wear*, no one but Jack knew she was covering the disappearance of the Granite Goddess. And who would leak those facts anyway? *Why? And why would anyone want to ship her and Scout to Lebanon? Why would the person send Michael there? What would that person—or the organization either behind the person or controlled by him—do to the three of them next? Were each of them on someone's hit list?*

Whoever had ordered Michael and her transported to Lebanon likely held the Granite Goddess hostage, too. But no one had asked for ransom money. *Why would someone want a supermodel, a reporter, and a fashion magazine editor, especially in a country heavily populated with Moslems who were forbidden to read such a rag or to socialize with persons in their occupations?* None of this computed to Chelsey, and that, too, rattled her.

CHAPTER 3
Arab Intrigues

<u>Beirut, Lebanon: August 12, 2015</u>

Smoke rings swirled above Prince Abdul El Fashid's forehead while he leaned back in a chair and propped his legs on the huge, mahogany Louis XIV desk that formed a citadel around him. The desk was part of the furniture his father had installed in his office, which housed wide, oak floor-to-ceiling bookcases, red and gold Persian carpets, and an array of tropical plants that dangled in front of the wall of windows that gave him a view of Beirut's shoreline, dappled with trees and houses that stretched to the water's edge. The prince held a palm pilot, and he furiously played a game where gargoyles ran after a man on a bicycle. To him, such games emulated life—always the chase, always the obstacles, always the adrenaline rush of winning.

Every minute or two, he puffed on the cigar lying in the ashtray by his in-box. The box held an uneven stack of papers at least eight inches high. It was four p.m., and he hadn't touched them. His father had wanted him to be a businessman. "So much money in oil and exports," the old man had claimed. "We can multiply our fortune, ten, a hundred, a thousand-fold." But although Abdul enjoyed the fruits of his wealth—he drove a Jaguar, a Mercedes, a Cessna and another small jet, threw lavish parties, wined and dined the most fascinating women, and decorated each abode he'd bought with top of the line décor—he truly preferred fiddling with computers and writing and reading poetry, especially by Czeslaw Milosz and Pablo Neruda. Often, he borrowed from the latter for wooing. "Dark butterfly, I love your joyful body" would melt even the coldest woman. Sometimes, he painted portraits, too. Such activities rattled his father. "Allah would ruin you," the king claimed. "Except you have already ruined yourself." It saddened Abdul to see how his father's greed for wealth had made him forget poetry, a traditional sign of masculinity in Arabic tradition. His grandfather, his mother's father, had been a renowned poet. As a child, he'd sit by his grandfather's feet and listen to the man recite poetry he'd written, rich, sensual verse laden with beautiful imagery about a universe beyond the stars, or lines describing a sliver of a moon reflecting off soft water.

Besides, the prince couldn't help his leanings. He simply had no head for business—that is, until this offer came from the strange, unworldly beings. And that had been pure luck. He'd been flying in his jet, when a shimmering, oval-shaped, platinum ship zoomed around him. The object had magnetized his instruments so his plane stopped but miraculously didn't fall from the sky. Then, the ship sprayed a huge laser ray into the cockpit, and with the lights, came two tall, shimmery, iridescent beings. Dazed at first, he could only stammer objections. He wondered if the beings were evil *jinn*, come to trick or destroy him. Perhaps they would drive him mad. Finally, he decided they must be some of those who serve Allah. Even if their high-pitched, squeaky voices threw him off at first, the beings were kind and their bodies pulsed and glowed with a beauty that made him almost forget how irritating their voices were. In fact, it was only their voices that failed to meet Abdul's expectations of how Allah's servants would appear. But no testimonies had claimed that Allah's angels spoke in mellow, full voices. So who was he to question their sounds? After the event, he reflected, of course, they were from Allah: They not only forged a deal with him—it was one that would pay him millions.

Suddenly, the phone on his desk buzzed, and he flinched. "Your Highness," his secretary Lorna Dune, a middle-aged British woman who had once served one of his father's other wives as the royal governess, announced, "a Mr. Ishmael el-Haddid is here."

Startled, Prince El Fashid dropped his palm pilot. It ricocheted off the corner of his desk and tumbled onto the carpet. "Shit!" He drew in his legs and scrambled to the floor.

"What was that, Your Grace?" Mrs. Dune gasped.

"Nothing." The prince, crawling now on his hands and knees, flipped over his palm pilot and frowned. He'd lost the game. He cleared his throat. Quickly he tapped on the glass to clear out the game page. "Send him in." The prince crawled back into his chair and exhaled loudly. Not only did he not like interruptions, he was not in the mood to see Ishmael.

The large man stomped into the huge office. The prince glanced up, noting how Ishmael's presence darkened the sunlit room, much like a storm cloud moving over a dessert. Once, when the prince was a rebellious youth, he had found Ishmael interesting. He was a commoner, and sheltered in a world of Arab royalty of more than a hundred brothers, sisters, and cousins, Abdul wanted to learn more about the common people. And although the man's manners were rough, Abdul didn't mind at first. But later, he wondered if the man weren't harsher with persons than he needed to be. So, recently, the prince dreaded seeing the swarthy man who smelled of curry and cheap Jade East. And now, because certainly, he couldn't trust any of his father's servants to keep the beings' orders confidential—especially from his father, he'd accepted having to associate with Ishmael as the downside of the new operation. So he would make the best of it. He smiled, stood, and held out a hand. "Good afternoon, Mr. el-Haddid." He picked up a carved, bronze box from his desk. "Cigar?"

Ishmael nodded, quickly shook the prince's hand, and grabbed a cigar, which he sniffed.

"Thank you, your Grace. Cuban?"

The prince nodded and swooped an arm toward the over-stuffed chair near his desk. "Sit down, and we shall talk. You've completed your mission, yes?"

Ishmael stretched back in the chair, his heavy trunk causing it to creak slightly. "Yes. I have them. Levine and the girl reporter."

"Chelsey McKay, is it not?"

Ishmael nodded and hesitated before he added, "And her dog."

The prince raised an eyebrow. "Her dog?" He frowned. "Did you say, 'her dog'?"

"I am sorry, your grace." Ishmael straightened his torso and leaned forward. "She insisted. It's tiny, scrawny—some German breed. But we confiscated her film."

The prince pursed his lips to feign a stern expression. In truth, he was delighted. "Yes, I should hope so. And if it is just a lap dog, it should cause no difficulty. These woman need their comforts." He smirked and flicked an ash. "Maybe American men would fare better by treating women as we do. Taking a lap dog on a job? Only a woman would do such a thing." He took a drag off his cigar. "But tell me, is she pretty? Might she be salable, too?"

Ishmael squinted, scratched his head, and shrugged. "Okay. A bit thin."

The prince laughed, a huge, throaty laugh. "You say that about all the Americans—even the Goddess."

"Goddess, hmmpf! These American women are all too skinny." Ishmael tilted his chin. "American men have no taste." The large man crossed his arms, frowned and shook his head.

"But the Goddess will bring the most cash from our, uh." The prince hesitated. He searched for a word but seemed not to quite find it. "From our, uh, contractors."

Then Ishmael laughed and leaned back in his chair. "You mean blackmailers, eh?"

The prince frowned. *How could the thug who sat before him be so audacious?* He had never met these beings with whom the prince negotiated. He had no understanding of politics, of a world view, or in this situation, an other-worldly view. He turned from Ishmael, stared at the rooftops reflecting the water, and cleared his throat. "Do not be so quick to judge, my friend. Some things are not what they seem."

"I meant no disrespect, Your Majesty." Ishmael's voice lowered. "It's just that this mission is so unusual. Stealing people is not my usual job."

Turning back to Ishmael, the prince raised an eyebrow, and crossed his arms. "We are not stealing these persons. We are not even borrowing them. We are transporting them to the place where they are meant to be. Besides, we have tried to treat both them and you fairly. You did no harm to these persons, correct?"

"Correct." Ishmael winced. "Other than sedating them."

"Doctors do that regularly." The prince shrugged. "I was assured these drugs would have no lasting harmful effects. They would merely keep these persons from reporting directions."

"Yes, Your Grace. But I am not used to sedating anyone other than our enemies. It seems these Americans do not know you."

"And are you not well compensated?"

"Yes, of course, Your Majesty." Ishmael straightened his back. "I'll just be glad to return to my usual duties."

"I am sure you will." The prince grimaced. "You have put them up at the Portemilio, correct? I will meet you there this evening. Set up reservations for the four of us at my table—the usual time. We will treat these Americans very kindly now."

CHAPTER 4
Musings

Chelsey looked out window, to where, just outside the building, a fig tree had begun to bloom. The huge narrow pines framed what was a prettier city than she'd imagined. She'd seen only photos of Beirut's ruins and hadn't anticipated seeing such a modern, bustling city. She'd also expected to see more evidence of the bombings. Perhaps, she'd relied too much on the descriptions P.J. O'Rourke's rendered for *Vacations in Hell*. At least, the city's ancient, stone beauty and the red, blue, yellow, even bright purple hijabs and gowns the women wore below—forming what looked like an aerial view of tropical flowers— were pleasant surprises.

Nonetheless, she couldn't yet come to terms with her situation. She was shocked, yes. But worse, she felt invaded. She wondered if she weren't suffering from PTSD, albeit a mild case. Along with confiscating her film, Ishmael had taken the notes she'd jotted about the Goddess. He'd taken her cell phone and tape recorder, too. Fortunately, he hadn't found the android buried in her makeup bag, and he'd ignored the small, old bible that once belonged to Erica, an elderly friend of her mother's. Chelsey didn't know why she'd brought it. She'd never taken it on a business trip before now. She didn't consider herself a religious person. Nevertheless, yesterday, she'd stuck it in her bag without thinking about it. Today, she was thankful she'd done so. She glanced at the leather-bound book on the end table, then shuffled over to the bed, plopped down, and picked up the book. Even if she weren't religious, on many days when she'd felt as helpless as today, she'd combed it for some comfort—often, reading the psalms gave her peace. And today, she was thankful she had the book as she thumbed through its thin pages. Perhaps it'd give her hope, inspire her about how to get out of this mess. Psalm 121 helped: "the Lord will protect thy going out and coming in from this day forth even now and forever more." Then, she scanned other pages. Here and there, Erica had circled verses with heavy red marker. Chelsey read a section that caught her:

"But in those days, after that tribulation, the sun shall be darkened, and the moon shall not give her light. And the stars of heaven shall fall, and the powers that are in heaven shall be shaken. And then shall they see the Son of man coming in the clouds with great power and glory." It was Mark 13:24-26.

She smiled. She vaguely remembered Erica, who smelled like dying roses and always wore her long, white hair twisted in a bun on the top of her head. Later, Neil had told Chelsey that Erica had once retained her connections with the Mafia. *How odd*, Chelsey thought, *for this woman who was always quoting scripture.* Perhaps the woman's words had affected Chelsey in some ways: at nearly 26 years old, she was still a virgin—and by choice, not by lack of opportunity.

Today, Chelsey wondered again about Erica's daily bible readings. It was a good story, perhaps. But she couldn't understand why the old woman had fingered these pages every night, how she'd found comfort in verses like these. In fact, now, reading them made Chelsey feel strange. It gave her goose bumps.

Afterwards, she slammed the book shut. She had to get moving. Somehow, she had to find Michael Levine and grill him about Isadora's whereabouts. Obviously, he knew something or Ishmael wouldn't have nabbed him. But why did he nab her? She knew nothing. It was crazy. She'd tried the door when she awoke. It was locked—apparently, from the outside. This, she thought, was highly irregular in a hotel. And apparently, Ishmael or Ishmael's boss had some connection with the owners. She thought about calling the house operator—or perhaps room service. She picked up the phone receiver. No dial tone. She tried punching "O" and the room service buttons. They didn't connect. Then, she looked at the back of the cradle. Of course, Ishmael had taken the cord. And no doubt, he'd done the same with Michael's. He'd probably locked up Michael in a suite nearby, but she was unsure how she could get to Michael—or at least, send a message to him.

Scout hopped into her lap and began licking a cut on the back of her left hand. She hadn't noticed it before. It was only a minor scratch—

perhaps she'd nicked it while she slept or maybe in her mad attempt to call out. She shoved the dog's head away from the sore and scratched him behind the ears. "It's okay, boy. How are you doing? I bet you're as groggy as me. Guess we were both drugged."

Cradling Scout, she stood and moved to the window again. Below, people milled in the street under what appeared to be an afternoon sun. Suddenly, Chelsey wondered what time it was. She glanced at the radio alarm. No electronic digits blinked. Apparently, Ishmael had unplugged it when he took the phone cord. She looked back at the street. Other than the unusually large number of soldiers that mixed with the throngs of street venders, it looked like a regular Mideast--albeit modern Mideast—city. She considered waving at the people—getting someone's attention. But she was five stories up. No one would see or hear her. Besides, she wasn't sure where Ishmael lurked. He might be waiting outside her room, listening for her to stir. Or perhaps, he was down in the lobby, keeping a lookout for anyone who might come in to rescue her. As if anyone could. Without her cell phone—or the hotel phone, she couldn't phone Jack. And even if she could reach him, how could he send anyone after her?

So she had to connect with Michael. But how?

She settled Scout on the bed. Then she returned to try prying open the window. If it opened even a bit, she might squeeze out of it—then maybe, maybe she could shimmy onto the ledge to the next room. Even if Michael weren't there, she could find help. Or perhaps someone below would see her and call the police. If Ishmael showed, he could do nothing. Too many people would see him—he couldn't ambush all of them in an alley. She checked the window for a latch. She could find nothing.

She turned from the window and paced from it to the door, turned, and repeated her walk. Scout hopped off the bed and followed her. "No, Boy, stay. Get back on the bed. There's nothing you can do."

The dog started whining, and she realized he needed to go out. Now, what was she to do? Even if she was so angry that she didn't care if Scout peed on the carpet, she knew the dog wouldn't. She'd trained him too well. But what could she do? She didn't know if Ishmael waited in the hallway with his .45. If he did, he might start shooting when she banged on the door. So she couldn't risk letting him out—and obviously, the dog wouldn't quit whining until she did. At first, she considered that Scout's whines might bring someone to the room. But no. If Ishmael had enough connections to lock the door from the outside, he'd ensured no one would open it. She sighed, looked around the room, and wished that dogs used litter boxes. Then, the thought inspired her: Perhaps she could get Scout to use the toilet. She'd known people who'd trained their cats to use the toilet. Of course, they likely didn't do so in a day. On the other hand, cats were often more obstinate than dogs. And today, she had no choice. She sighed. This wasn't going to be easy. "Come here, Boy." She patted one of her legs and backed into the bathroom, motioning for the dog to follow her. The dog stared at her and sat down. Whimpering still, he refused to move toward her or the door.

"C'mon Scout. You can go pee-pee here." Now, she patted both of her legs as she backed up.

The dog wouldn't budge. He wrinkled his brow, stared and whined. She went to him, and careful not to press upon his abdomen, she picked him up by wrapping her fingers around his outer ribcage. She carried him, legs flailing, into the bathroom.

Scout still whined when she lifted the toilet lid, picked up the dog, and positioned his legs on the seat. "It's okay, Boy, do it here." First, his back paws slid backwards, hit the tank and started to fall off the seat. She shoved them back in place, toward the bowl. Once she positioned them, the front ones slid, again, almost slipping off the rim. She gently pushed them back. Scout fell forward, nearly sliding into the water. Finally, she bent over and stretched herself over the dog, held his back paws in place with her hands, pressed her torso over him to wedge the front ones between her thighs and the seat.

"Come on, Boy, go." Scout looked up at her and wrinkled his forehead. He looked as if he were in pain. Then, the dog started whimpering.

"Come on, Scout."

The dog whimpered still.

She sighed. "Okay. Probably too weird for you. Let's try the shower." She lifted the dog and reached for the sliding door. After she slid back the door a little and glanced at the shower, she grinned. She drew the door farther back. Yes! Ishmael hadn't seen the phone in the shower stall. Its cord was intact. She placed the dog in the shower, shut the door, and turned on the nozzle. Scout growled at first, but finally, he urinated.

She punched in the number to the front desk. "Hello, I'm not sure which room I'm in. But I came here with two gentlemen, and I need to contact one of them, who's staying in another room."

"Madame, you are in room 524." The clerk's voice contained an incipient tone as if he smirked as he spoke. She was sure he figured she was a prostitute. Still, he remained polite and dutiful, because then, he asked, "And what is the other gentleman's name?"

"Michael Levine."

"Levine, Levine. I'm sorry Madame, but no one by that name is registered here."

"Perhaps it's under Ishmael."

"Ishmael Levine?" The clerk's voice raised in disbelief.

"No. I don't know his last name." "Madame, I assure you. There are many Ishmaels here. That name is quite common in Beirut." The man sighed. It seemed he thought she was a moron.

Chelsey bit her lip to control her rage. Finally, she spoke. "Listen:

Do you have a record of two rooms being rented by the same person at about say ten last night? We came in late—not many people were registering then."

"Let me check."

I hope Ishmael hasn't put the clamp on the front desk, too, she thought and began rapping her fingers on the tile wall. After what seemed like two hours, the clerk returned. While she waited, she stared at the shower nozzle. It reminded her of when a doctor gave her anesthetic for an operation on her spine. That was when the strange dreams began. Although she was merely eight years old, she dreamed of being abducted and taken to a space ship hovering over a field of daffodils. She remembered feeling as frightened in those dreams as she did today.

The clerk's voice startled her. "Yes, two rooms were rented by a Mr. Ishmael el-Haddid at 10:13 last night. Rooms 524 and 525."

"Could you connect me to 525?"

"I'll try." He connected her, and the phone rang. And rang. And rang. Yes, apparently, Ishmael had cut Michael's line, too. At least, now, she knew where he was. It was just a matter of getting to him. And she was grateful that the desk clerk didn't withhold information. That meant she could reach Jack. She dialed the front desk again and asked the clerk to dial *The Globe*'s number. Of course, static flared and cut into their connection.

"Jack—can you hear me?"

"Chelsey? Where are you? Why haven—"

"I've been kidnapped, Jack—no kidding. Levine, too—

"Talk louder. I can—"

"KIDNAPPED! LEVINE, too," she yelled. "By some Arab named Ishmael."

"Kidnapped?"

"Yeah—we're in Leban—"

The static rose to a crescendo, breaking up her words, so she was unsure if Jack heard the location. Surely he could tell by the connection she'd phoned from overseas. And how many countries sounded anything like Lebanon? Perhaps the return number would show on *The Globe*'s phone. On the other hand, perhaps it didn't appear this time, and perhaps Jack hadn't heard her last line at all. At least, he knew she'd been abducted. Whether that would help her escape, she was unsure. Nonetheless, knowing she'd reached someone raised her confidence, which had plummeted well below sea level. Now, she had to figure how to contact Michael. She hung up the phone and stepped back into the suite. Facing the window, she tried to remember which way the numbers went. Was 525 to her right or across the hall? Her memory had blurred. Not only had she been drowsy from the flight, but the drug Ishmael had apparently slipped her had jumbled her memory, too. Thinking clearly had come slowly for her that morning, but finally, she realized that if Ishmael took the phone cords and locked them inside, he likely wasn't outside the door. She decided to risk making a racket: She knotted her hands into fists and pounded on the wall to her right, where 525 would be, if it were on this side of the hall.

No answer.

"Michael!" She yelled and pounded harder till the Mondrian reproductions seemed they'd shake out of their frames. In fact, she slammed her fists against the wall until her water glass rattled on the end table. Still, no one responded. She decided that obviously, then, 525 was across the hall. Or perhaps, it was indeed next door, and Michael was unconscious. She wondered if Ishmael had drugged him and if Michael lay in a coma, smothering face-down in his saliva—or in his blood. Or perhaps, she reconsidered, Ishmael had taken Michael somewhere, maybe to some alley somewhere, or along some desert highway, badly beaten or even dead.

Then she heard someone fiddling with her door. She grabbed Scout, and almost stumbling over one of her bags, fled into the bathroom and locked it. She looked at the phone, unplugged its cord, looked around to find somewhere to hide it, gave up, and stuffed it into her bra. It pressed hard against her breast and formed awkward lumps in her shirt. Worried that Ishmael had been waiting in the hallway after all, that he might have heard her hammering on the wall and calling for Michael, she pressed an ear to the bathroom door. She was fairly certain she'd be able to recognize Ishmael's heavy gate and his cough. But she didn't hear heavy footsteps or any coughing. Nevertheless, she heard someone.

"Ms. McKay," a man called softly. "Chelsey?" His voice didn't sound foreign. It didn't sound like Ishmael's, but she wasn't sure. She hadn't heard Ishmael speak softly before. She worried that perhaps it was indeed him, that he was trying to seduce her into opening the door. Then again, she considered it could be the front desk clerk, who'd run upstairs because perhaps someone had complained about her pounding. But the desk clerk's voice had sounded foreign. He'd spoken in broken English, too. For a minute, she tried to remember if she'd given the clerk her name. But in her panic, she couldn't remember. Finally, she concluded she'd have to at least see who was there. Nonetheless, she felt her heart beat fast and her fingers quivered when she cracked the door.

It was Michael Levine.

CHAPTER 5
Michael's Story

Sweating and nearly breathless, he sputtered, "We need to scram—now." He ran fingers through his hair. Chelsey noticed how thick his hair was, even though he had to be at least fifty, maybe 55. But his lines ran deep and the circles under his eyes seemed darker than when she last saw him, especially when he ordered, "Grab what you need."

She said nothing but picked up her bags and put Scout back in the carrier. He didn't fight her but whimpered. She dug through her bag and pulled on a blonde wig. That way, if Ishmael returned, he wouldn't easily recognize her. Michael looked at her and grinned. After they left the room, she whispered, "I wonder when Ishmael will return."

"No telling." He clutched her elbow and steered her down the hall and to the stairwell. "Can't risk the elevator. Doubt that tub of lard will take the stairs."

After Michael hailed a cab and they headed eastward, he explained he'd found a phone in his bathroom, too, and had called room service, claiming something had gone wrong with his lock. "We were lucky," he said. Apparently, the night managers don't talk much to the day clerks." While the cab sped down the boulevard, she watched Michael slip a piece of gum from his inside pocket. He offered her a stick, but she declined. Her stomach churned now, so she wanted no treats. Just information. "Why did they kidnap us?"

He glanced at the cabby, pulled down the divider, leaned toward her, and whispered, "I'm not sure. But perhaps it's because I know about Isadora."

"What?" Chelsey leaned toward him. "Where is she?"

"She's here." He frowned and squinted at the window.

"Where?"

He sighed and looked back at her. "Exactly where, I don't know. But she's in Beirut. And the same folks kidnapped her."

"Why did they take me?"

"Apparently, they didn't know how much you knew."

She smirked. "I would've known more if you'd met me."

He grimaced. "I would've met you if Asli wouldn't have grabbed me first."

"Asli?"

"Ishmael's cohort."

Chelsey crossed her arms and leaned back in the seat. "What else do you know about Isadora?"

He glanced at her, looked away, and then stared at her eyes, as if he were trying to see beyond them. "This is off the record, okay?"

Chelsey nodded. "Of course."

"She's involved with a prince from Saudi Arabia. His father set him up in a branch here. He exports tobacco—and who knows what else, maybe humans and drugs—from here to Saudi Arabia."

"A prince? Why would he need to work?"

Michael shrugged. "I'm not sure how much actual 'work' he performs. He seems to have a lot of spare time for Isadora. Oddly enough, he's bought her diamonds and rubies, even set her up in a suite—from which, as I understand it, she can't leave without him. But he hasn't made any physical moves on her. She called and told me about him. She's hung up on him and wonders if he's gay."

"Maybe he wants to marry her."

"You might be right." Michael grinned. "Most Arab men I've known go after women as sexual conquests. But they want their wives to be 'pure.' Of course, Isadora would be quite a trophy for a wife."

"Why then, such a covert operation? Why did Ishmael kidnap her?"

"Ishmael works for the prince. For some reason, it seems the prince doesn't want his involvement with Isadora known—at least, not yet. I've heard he's involved with one of the political groups here, too. Maybe that has something to do with it." Michael shrugged. "But I really only know Isadora's take on all this. Maybe something else is going on."

"Which political group?"

"Who knows?" he shrugged. "There are hundreds of them here."

Chelsey leaned back in her seat and stared out the side window. Something seemed awry. But then, she didn't know this country and knew even less about the Arab mind, even if she'd read about it.

"You know." Michael patted a shoulder. "You look a lot like your mother. And she was beautiful."

She glanced back at him. "Thanks, but I'm not much like her."

"That's probably good."

She looked at the ocean in the rear view mirror. "Where are we going?"

"To Anwar."

"Why?"

Suddenly, a car popped up behind them. It seemed to gain on them. Chelsey watched it move closer while she talked with Michael.

"There's a U.S. Embassy there," he said. "You can seek asylum."

"Asylum? I haven't done anything wrong."

"No. But think of your environment." He grinned. "That way, you'll be safe."

Still eying the rear-view mirror, she squeezed Michael's arm. "That is, if we make it. Look in the mirror."

The car was a limo. And it continued gaining on them. Two dark, bearded men sat in the front seat. But with the dark windshield, neither Chelsey nor Michael could recognize either of the men's faces. Michael knocked on the partition then raised it. Holding up a thumb, he yelled,

"Step on it! Speed up!" Michael turned and stared at the car behind the cab. "Have you seen these men before? At the airport maybe?"

Chelsey shrugged. "If I did, I didn't notice them."

The cab zoomed ahead. But the limo accelerated, too. Michael directed the cabby to turn off on a highway, accelerate even more down the winding path that led further outside the city. Chelsey turned and squinted at the car to see if Ishmael drove it. She couldn't tell even when the limo moved closer.

"Could we switch back or something? Maybe it isn't him. Did he have time to check for us?

Michael directed the cabby to turn on a trail in a median. The cab lunged over bumps, shook and shimmied until they headed back west. Wondering if it would turn around to stay on their tail, Chelsey watched the limo. It stayed in the eastbound lane. She sighed and leaned her head back on the seat. "Thank God."

***

After they returned to the highway heading east, Chelsey asked Michael where Isadora was—precisely. She didn't want to go to the Embassy—at least, not without seeing Isadora. She arched her back.

He scratched his head and shifted his eyes away from her stare. "I'm not sure. I haven't talked with her for a week. Then, she was staying in the prince's household.

"In Beirut?"

"I'm not sure about that, either. He has more than one here. And then, of course, his main palace is in Saudi Arabia."

"So she could be there."

Michael shook his head. "She said Lebanon."

Chelsey watched the ripples of skin around Michael's eyes. He was hiding something, she knew it. But what? Why didn't she trust him, even after he released her from Ishmael's cage? She leaned back in her seat again. "I need to see her before I leave."

"What? After all this?" He exhaled loudly. "Are you crazy?"

"Perhaps." She smiled. "But I must talk with her."

"Maybe you're more like your mother than I thought." Michael frowned then turned away from her and stared out the window.

Chelsey glared at him, settled back in her seat, and closed her eyes. Other than at the fashion show, she hadn't seen Michael since she was a kid. About those times, her memories blurred, although she remembered how he'd affected her mother. Her mother had liked Michael—no doubt, too much. She'd laughed and her step seemed to bounce after every time he'd phoned her. And once, when he came to visit her mother in Kansas City, after they'd left her father in Alberta, Canada, the three of them had gone to a park.

It'd been an overcast day in early spring. Daffodils had bloomed, but most flowers hadn't. The trees had barely begun to bud. Her mother had run ahead, turned back, jogged backwards and stuck out her tongue to tease Michael. Then, later, they flew a kite together, the three of them running through Loose Park, their hair flying, the wind hitting their cheeks. Those were happy days. But now, thinking of them made Chelsey wistful. She often felt wistful when she remembered her mother, especially on an overcast day when clouds hung low. She'd been so young when she died. And sometimes when Chelsey would hear a sad, haunting folk song about lost love, especially by Alison Krauss, she'd picture her mother, sometimes laughing, but more often, with a sad, haunting expression. In fact, with her sad, deep-set eyes, Alison looked much like Chelsey's memory of her mother's face.

She looked back at Michael. He'd stayed in shape, yes. But he wasn't the man she remembered. Jowls had started to form—just slightly, and the creases around his eyes had grown deeper. Even with his shock of hair, it seemed his forehead was higher—and then, the wisps of gray framing his face added years to his image. Why hadn't the jerk married her mother? It wasn't that Chelsey saw him as much of a father-figure. But he'd made her mother laugh. If he'd stayed with her, she'd never been murdered. Thinking about this, Chelsey began to feel resentful again.

And she couldn't afford that now. Not with both their lives—and who knew how many other lives and what else—at stake. So she glanced at Michael, then looked out the window, and watched the street whiz by while the bay slipped further and further away, and she tried not to think of anything. She said nothing, but tapped her fingers in her right hand on a knee. Suddenly, Michael pressed a hand on the back of her neck and began rubbing it gently. At first, Chelsey flinched, then she slowly relaxed. Something about Michael's touch was reassuring— even if she barely knew him. Even though she didn't especially trust him, either, she didn't feel threatened by his touch. Perhaps because she had known him so long ago, it comforted her. Perhaps because he was old enough to be her father, she felt at ease. Nonetheless, she continued looking out the window. Then, he spoke in a low, confiding voice. "I know you probably hate me—and probably should." He sighed. "Look, I loved your mother. But I was so young. You know, I was more than ten years younger than she was."

Chelsey looked back at him. "Why was that important?"

He frowned. "I'm not saying it was. It isn't that I was too young for her. It's that I was too young—and irresponsible—to handle a family then. I was just a pup trying to build a career."

Chelsey smirked. "I guess you succeeded."

"Guess so. But I gave up a lot. And believe me, if I'd known what was going on in your mom's life, I would've brought both of you to New York."

"She didn't tell you about Jules?"

"Some. But I thought she was happy. I had no idea what he was doing to her."

"You should've talked to me."

Michael almost laughed when he tossed back his head. "You were only three."

"But I knew Jules was evil. He took away my dog."

Michael smiled. "No wonder you brought your Doberman with you."

Chelsey glanced down at Scout. He'd been unusually quiet. "Yeah. I take him on any long trip."

Michael drew back his hand and patted her right arm. "Good for you. Probably a good idea." He glanced out the other window. "We've probably got enough of a lead on them. I doubt they'll figure out where we're going. At least, not for a while. Maybe we can stop and eat. You're probably hungry, aren't you?"

"Yes," she lied. "But I won't go to the Embassy till I see Isadora."

"You just might have to." Michael frowned again, then he looked pensive. "And maybe we can get help to bring her there, too."

She stared at him a minute then turned to look out the window at the olive tree groves now whisking by. If they stopped to eat, she might get a chance to ditch Michael. She meant it when she said she wasn't leaving without interviewing Isadora. If she had to leave him dining alone so she could track down Isadora, so be it. Michael wouldn't be the first man she'd left alone in a restaurant.

CHAPTER 6
Beyond the Stars

The beings in the lab shimmered with iridescent glows. Their bodies reached more than seven-feet tall, and with their wide hip joints, they were shaped like upside-down toilet plungers, capped with heads that emulated light-bulbs above narrow, nearly non-existent shoulders. And the light that emanated from them made them appear to glow like uranium, partially because the light their auras emitted reflected off the white walls in the huge, spotless laboratory extending about twenty feet high to a ceiling with a large, dome skylight nearly fifty feet in diameter. The skylight allowed the beings to study the skies. With their telescopic eyes, they could see 93 million light years into the heavens.

Two of the beings huddled together, intent upon probing some substance through a microscope. The taller one peered through its glass. "These specimens have nearly identical Deoxyribonucleic Acid—that's DNA to you," he remarked. "Incredible. It is almost identical. How odd." His eyes were set in larger sockets than the short ones, and as he spoke in a whistling Serkerpian voice, the thick bristles above his eye sockets bobbed up and down. All Serkerpian eyes were dark, like huge, teardrop-shaped, onyx settings. Instead of distinguishing them by color,

Serkerpians differentiated eyes by variations in the sockets and in their eyebrows. Some sockets were more circular, less tear-shaped.

"Dardiel, let me see," the shorter one interjected. The few bristles above his eyes barely moved. And even if they had moved, they were so pale, they were nearly imperceptible.

"In a minute." Dardiel pursed his lips. "I'm still examining it—and I must calculate—"

"Then project it on the screen, Dardiel," the short one huffed as much as he could huff, considering that his thin, high-pitched voice, like the voices of all Serkerpians sounded akin to a teakettle's whistle. "We both must examine this. We can't risk an error now."

"Okay, okay. You're so impatient." Dardiel pressed buttons on the side of the microscope and a large blue and yellow hologram appeared on the screen above the microscope. "Two creatures, unrelated. Hmmm. We've never had these results from two humanoids before, have we, Liwet?"

Liwet rubbed an eye socket and shook his head. "Not in the 22,000 samples you've taken—unless, of course, they were from family members."

"And these two just met." Dardiel rubbed a socket with the back of one of his wings. "In fact, the prince's brutish go-for brought them together. Highly irregular." Liwet yawned while Dardiel continued. "But I must research some more—perhaps it is possible. It may be that these specimens are distant cousins who don't know of their DNA relationship." Dardiel stared at the video screen for some time. "Certainly, they are closer than cousins. See, the red, the green, the blue areas—almost identical."

"Hmmm." Liwet frowned. "Perhaps that prince has conned us. Perhaps he's sending us those who cannot populate a world, those who would create a race of raging lunatics. He may be trying to trick us."

Dardiel laughed. "I am not so sure any earthling wouldn't do that— especially after a few generations of mating within their species."

Now Liwet glared. "But we told him to pluck only the best of the species—the most comely, the most peaceful, the least violent, the least warlike—those who would create a new Heaven."

"Perhaps we should have bargained with Buddhists?" Dardiel smiled so broadly, his bushy eyebrows became one furry ridge across his forehead. He was quite proud of his expertise in interplanetary studies, especially of religions.

"Right." Liwet fluttered his wings in irritation. "And just how many of them own their own jets and go dashing around in the stratosphere?"

"Besides." Dardiel patted one of his colleague's shoulders. "Emeth gave the order, Liwet. He knows what he is doing—even if we don't."

"Hmmphf. I still don't understand why he did not allow that last meteor to destroy earth and all those violent humanoids. Look at them now—they're battling around the Holy Land, of all places."

"But, my friend, it is written—"

"I know. I know." Liwet's wings fluttered again. "And I shouldn't question. But I know this: Those two beings should never mate."

"I doubt they will, Liwet. I doubt—"

Suddenly, a huge explosion somewhere above the skylight shook the lab and sent the image on the video screen into wild, uneven rotations. Dardiel and Liwet stared at each other, then they began reeling and wobbling, till finally they grabbed each other's arms to steady their balance. Each of them could see the terror in the other's eyes. "What was that?" Liwet's sockets grew wide. "Where did it come from?"

"I don't know." Dardiel sighed. "But I don't think it's wise to question Emeth. Especially when we are in this ship not very far from earth—and truly, a million miles from nowhere."

They held on and steadied each other for awhile, until the floor of the lab and its walls became quiet. The video images became steady now, and the twosome went back to examining them. It had been a long, tedious winter. Both were eager to finish this project and leave the galaxy. But the rest of the afternoon, they worked on, testing the DNA, testing the hair follicles to learn everything about the earthlings.

CHAPTER 7
The Chase

The voices inside Ishmael's head told him he was a bad person. They were high-pitched, squeaky voices that simply wouldn't leave him alone. "Kidnapper!" they shrieked. "Allah will damn you!" How could he respond to them? Yes, he'd become a kidnapper. On the other hand, he'd abducted only infidels. And he did it as his duty to his employer. *Yes, the money was good.* He desperately needed the money, with three teenagers, a wife, her sister, and a mistress to support. Didn't that mitigate his sin somewhat? But often, other voices, voices from inside his soul, sent him queries. So he wondered what the prince planned to do with these persons. The prince had spoken of contractors—*but who were those contractors?* Why hadn't he introduced them to him, or at least, told him their names? *Why was this operation so covert?* With these questions reverberating in his head, he drove in a daze, ignoring the sunny skies and winds sweeping from the south, swerved into the hotel lot, parked his BMW, then marched back into the lobby. The idiot day clerks were at the front desk, so he nodded at them quickly and dashed to the elevator before they ambushed him with more harassing questions. Inside the elevator, a plump, gray-haired woman who stank of stale Estee Lauder clutched a black toy poodle. He tipped his hat to her, turned and watched the buttons flicker. The woman's dog yapped and snarled. The yapper reminded him of Scout. *Why had that reporter brought a dog with her?* he wondered. The prince was right—no professional man would do that. *Perhaps she believed the dog would protect her.* Ishmael chuckled at that idea. *Such a puny dog— protection, hah!* Then he entertained an idea: He'd befriend the dog. He fumbled through his pockets for some tidbit, a cracker, something he could slip to the dog when he returned to the room. Then, the dog would certainly not attack him. It'd foil any plan this Chelsey woman might have about sic-ing her dog on him.

He found nothing. So Ishmael rode the elevator up a floor, where the woman and poodle disembarked. He pressed the lobby button, hurried into a gift shop, bought doggy treats, and engaged the elevator again. *This would be better.* That way, Chelsey wouldn't complain the way many dog-owners did when a person gave their pets scraps. Ishmael whistled as he strode down the hall of the fifth floor. Yes, what an ingenious idea—befriending the dog. Still humming when he unlocked the door, he looked around for Scout's carrier. He could find it nowhere. He scanned the suite. "Hello?" he called while he knocked on the bedroom door. No answer. He tried the bathroom, still maintaining his polite call. No answer. Then he stomped back into the suite. He scanned the room. No clothes hung on the hangers in the small armoire. Chelsey's bags were gone. So was the dog carrier. Now other voices raged inside him, calling him "Fool! Idiot!" Yes, he was as stupid as the day clerks. He dropped the doggy treats into his pocket and flew out of the suite and across the hall to the room where he'd locked in Levine.

In less than five minutes, he was back in his car and whirling madly down the highway. The voices attacked again. *Where could they have gone? Who'd let them out? Undoubtedly, Room Service.* But he'd hung "Do Not Disturb" signs on each door, and they were still in place. *No way would the maids open the door. No way could either of them have phoned the front desk.* Oh, he'd been such a fool to leave them unguarded. Ishmael had to find Chelsey and Levine. No way could he tell the prince about their escape.

Even though his mind became a whirling dervish, he speculated where they might have fled. *To Isadora?* But Levine didn't yet know exactly where she was. *Or did he?* He rapped his fingers on the steering wheel and glanced across the desert landscape. The winds blew stronger here and now stirred up dust that formed brown clouds encompassing him. Maybe they were hiding back in Beirut. *No. Certainly, Levine would be smart enough to realize the prince's staff could cover that city in less than an hour. Then, where did they go?* Ishmael wondered, and he worried even more. *Maybe Levine knew someone in the city.* He pulled out a cigar from his glove compartment, tore off the end with his teeth, lit it, and thought some more. At first, he thought the prince had sent him after Levine and Chelsey because they'd tried to locate Isadora.

But it had to be more complex than that. Otherwise, the prince would likely have had someone take them into the desert, maybe shoot them. *But who were the contractors?* It made sense they wanted Isadora, a glamorous model. *But why a small-time reporter and an aging magazine editor? A woman's magazine at that?* For some reason, these two were special—the prince asked for them specifically. He'd planned to dine with them, as if they were foreign dignitaries. And now, he, Ishmael had lost them. Now, he was in trouble. *Big trouble.* Plus, the prince hadn't seemed too happy to see him lately, either, the moody bastard, him with his poetry and painting. Once the girlish prince learned of this fiasco, he'd become like a raging shrew going through menopause. Then Ishmael could kiss his paycheck—and who knows? maybe his life—goodbye. His life—oh, he needed some safe harbor, some asylum. *Asylum? Asylum--that was it.* Probably Levine was shuttling Chelsey to the Embassy. But it was all the way in Anwar— much too far to walk. Ishmael had taken their money. So how could they have hailed a cab? Ishmael puffed on the cigar again, then patted his revolver in his pocket. *How didn't matter. Why didn't matter.* He had to find those two and get them back to the Portemilio before dinner time, of that, he was sure.

"Oh shit!" he said aloud. He'd forgotten to phone for dinner reservations. Allah was not smiling upon him today. He pulled onto the shoulder, slid his cell phone out of his sports jacket, and started to dial the Portemilio's front desk. He glanced at his watch and stopped. It was 2:30 already, and the prince always dined at eight. He needed more time--at least, an extra hour. Okay, he'd have to risk it--he dialed and made a nine o'clock reservation. Certainly, the *maitre d'* would set up the prince at his private booth in the bar area. If Ishmael was lucky, the prince would spot some woman who'd distract him from the time.

But lately, it seemed Ishmael was rarely lucky. Ever since his fortieth birthday, his luck had turned sour. The prince hadn't seemed happy with him for the past three years. And the last two months, he seemed especially irritated with him. So he couldn't risk upsetting him now. He stared at the rock along the highway and thought for a few minutes more. Today, he'd have to make his luck. He pressed the phone pad for his addresses. *Shahara? No. Not classy enough. Even if Ishmael liked her looks, the prince would think her too hefty, too dowdy. Hoda? No. Too pale. Too intellectual. Fatima? Ah yes, Fatima. She smelled like melons, or perhaps, an exotic tea, and her long silk skirts seemed to float around her wide, curved hips. Her long, dark hair and succulent lips would surely lure the prince to her table. And then, her seductive eyes and a voice that flowed like honey would keep him entranced.* He punched in her number.

"Hello, My Sweet, My Lovely." He grinned as he looked at the windshield.

"Ishmael?" She sounded irritated. "What do you want?"

"I have a charming job for you tonight, my dearest."

"Hmmphf." She coughed. "Another foreigner for me to entertain?"

"Oh no. Much better—"

"I should hope so. That last one—the Brit! Such a cheapskate!"

"Oh no, not a Brit. This man's a prince. An Arabian prince."

"A prince? Really?"

"Ah yes—and he loves the ladies."

"So why haven't you set me up with him before?"

"He has always been entangled with other women before."

"Why isn't he now?"

"Oh, he's lonely and heart-broken now," Ishmael lied. "His latest love has left him. He probably did not give her enough attention. Working too hard, I suppose."

"So why would he give me attention?"

"Like I said, he's lonely now. And he's learned from his errors. He's also a poet."

"So he's brooding?"

"No—no. He's looking for another love."

"A poet? So he's broke?"

"Not at all." Ishmael shook his head and crossed his arms.

He stared at the road ahead. "No—no. He *is* a prince—a real one. His father's set him up in business. Big oil family. Great tipper."

Ishmael could hear Fatima's heavy sigh.

"And he'll pay well? How much?"

"I will pay you."

"How much?"

"Ten thousand riyals."

"For a night?"

"For about an hour—maybe two. You need only talk with him, occupy him. Till I can get there."

"Hmmm?" She was silent for a few seconds. "And you'll pay me when you arrive?"

"Oh, yes. But you will be so charmed, you won't want the pay."

"Don't count on it."

Ishmael sighed. At least, he'd gained an hour, maybe two. Now, he had to find Levine and the girl. *Who knows?* Maybe he'd bribe them to meet the prince, too. Or maybe they'd want to meet the prince out of curiosity. At this point, Ishmael realized he'd lost control to this situation. Well, fine. But he had to pull everything back together. Apparently, these Americans couldn't be cowed as easily as he'd anticipated. Who would've guessed they would have enough courage to break out of their rooms when he could've been outside their doors, waiting for them? None of the old tricks worked anymore. He'd have to use deadly force to intimidate them. He wouldn't merely pat his revolver. He must start shooting it, if merely at the sky. He swerved back onto the highway and headed east toward Anwar.

CHAPTER 8
Back in Beirut

After Ishmael left, the prince leaned back in his chair and resumed his game for a few more minutes. But it no longer held his attention. His mind repeatedly returned to fantasies about the American reporter. Even if he could have any woman in Beirut, in fact, in Saudi Arabia, American women intrigued him the most, perhaps because they challenged him. His lines of poetry, even those he borrowed from Neruda, did not work so readily on them. *All that independence made them too cold*, he thought. *They had forgotten about romance.*

But this one might be different. Yes, surely she would be different. After all, she made her living with words. She must love words. This woman, he was sure, must be fiery, passionate. For a woman, she was so brave to come here—to try to find that ice queen Isadora. Most likely, this reporter was beautiful, too, especially if Ishmael did not find her that attractive. Ishmael had such rustic taste in women, the prince contended, *always he liked the heavy-lidded, overly-seductive ones, the earth mothers, never the sophisticated, slender Western types.* Indeed, he would never send Ishmael to select a woman for him—not even for an hour.

For a few minutes, he fiddled with the papers toppling over the edges of his in-box. Shipping contracts awaiting his signature, invoices awaiting checks, requests for price lists, invitations to business breakfasts and luncheons, all boring affairs. *Why was business so boring?* He could not keep his mind on it. It bored him even more than much of life bored him. In fact, most of his life—no matter how exciting he had tried to make it—had become, admittedly, boring. *So empty, a bowl overturned after a huge feast. That is, until lately.* Things had picked up since he met the otherworldly beings. At first, of course, they had scared him. His knees had trembled and his fingers froze on the instrument panel. He had almost wet his pants. The ship had appeared so quickly—out of nowhere. Then the laser ray had swelled into his cockpit. And the beings followed. He wondered where they came from—those shimmery beings with the obsidian eyes and the huge, white wings that swooped around his head when they fluttered in. He had thought they were angels. In fact, he was still uncertain they were not. Later, when they contacted him, not actually by speaking but through some sort of telepathy, they were so peaceful, so calm, as if every day, they contacted and bargained with princes, that their signals made him relax. They had sent out an aura that calmed him as if it were Darvon or Demerol. Even later, he reflected that they probably seemed calm because they came from some other planet, because they did not have to deal with this cut-throat world.

He shoved the papers aside and pulled out a lower drawer. Underneath more papers, he had hidden his book of Neruda's twenty love poems. Ah yes—he would memorize a couple of lines for the American woman tonight. If she was a reporter, she would likely enjoy hearing literature. He pulled the book into his lap and thumbed through a few pages.

"Who are you, who are you?" he read. *How appropriate for this situation*, he thought. *Almost psychic.* But then, the words would not quite create the ambiance he wanted to create. He flipped a few more pages. "Girl lithe and tawny." Oh yes, certainly she was. Ishmael said she was young, yes, less than twenty-four. " . . . the sun that forms the fruits, that plumps the grains, that curls seaweeds filed your body with joy, and your luminous eyes and your mouth that has the smile of the water." *Ah yes—these would do.* He would switch the words around a little. *But the images—yes, so sensual. Indeed, they would work. And the curtained, candlelit booth would help create the right ambiance.* He would order it set up with flowers—which kinds? *Roses, no not yet. Something more exotic. Hmmm—orchids, maybe? Yes, orchids— perhaps orange ones with brown rims.* Maybe a day or two later, he would send a dozen roses. Surely, she would respond. And tonight— after likely living in fear these last hours—ah yes! She would love him. Perhaps she would not be like the other Americans. She would love him, he was sure, almost sure. At least, she would certainly feel some attraction for him. He wondered if he should select an evening gown and have it sent to her room. But then, he did not know her size. And if he sent too large a size, she would be insulted. On the other hand, if it were too small, she could not wear it, and that, too, would likely make her angry. Either way, he could lose.

He sighed. *Women—so intriguing, but oh, so temperamental.* At times like these especially, he wished his mother were still alive. She had been the opposite of his father—she was quiet, calm. In fact, Abdul sometimes wondered if his father's overbearing nature had not driven her to her grave. If she were alive, she would calm him now. She would know how to appease the American woman. His mother had been blessed with a knack for sensing people's needs. Usually, she could keep even his fiery father calm. He dropped the book to his desk and stared at the bookcases. They were dusty and in one corner, a spider had woven a web that looked like gauze. Gauze, such a fragile fabric, he thought. She would look good in a fine, thin fabric, especially if she had auburn hair. Perhaps he could dispatch a tailor, a dressmaker. He jabbed a button on his phone and buzzed Ms. Dune. "Your Majesty?"

"Remember that dressmaker I hired to outfit Isadora?"

"Yes."

"Please call her and send her to the Portemilio, Room 524. Have her bring silks and satins, beautiful deep maroons and blues, flowing fabrics, fine—almost transparent."

"I'll try, Your Grace." She sighed. "But I'm not sure I can reach her. Usually she needs a day's notice."

"It must be done today." He lowered his tone to make his voice sound sterner. "Immediately. I will double her usual fee. And buzz me once you have reached her and made the arrangements." She would set it up. The woman was old but had an excellent rapport with clients and workers. And the American Ms. McKay would be so grateful, perhaps even awed, he knew it.

He stood and stretched, then gazed out across the city. Beirut. *Such a noisy place. Too many people. Too many soldiers. Too many cars and trucks and buses rattling down streets.* At first, the city had intrigued him, but now, it too, had become boring. *But oh—tonight, the sea was lovely.* It called to him, made him yearn to go away to the country again, to Crete, that island off Greece, to work steadily on his poetry, to write undisturbed for hours, then to swim in the sea with his beloved—the one true love he had not yet found in his twenty-nine years—ah yes! This was the life he needed, a life like Neruda lived during his years in Italy, a life filled with open hours that would be so much richer than those crammed with meetings and phone calls and too many people to see. He could give up his video games and technology just to live a quiet life in the country with his love, just as Neruda had.

His phone buzzed. He pressed a button to activate the speaker. "Yes? Did you reach her?"

"Not yet, Your Grace. I left a message. But I wanted to remind you that you meet with your father and the Russian general at five-thirty."

"Ah yes." He inhaled deeply and frowned. They would share another miserable round of drinks—vodka no doubt—with the Russian haggling for discounts, wanting oil so cheap they would make no money. And his father would argue, haggle him down, under his breath reminding the prince, See—this is how it is done—listen and learn, flailing his arms till his loose sleeves flapped in the prince and general's faces, all the while both of the older men getting drunker and louder, each of them trying to flirt with the waitress, taking turns pinching her buttocks. But it was not a meeting he could shrug off. "Thank you, Ms. Dune. Please continue to ring up the dressmaker."

He glanced at his watch. Four-thirty. He punched Ishmael's number. No answer. The recording said he'd switched it off. *How odd*, the prince thought. *Ishmael never switched off his cell phone. The man planned his life around his cell phone—it was his prized possession. He took it everywhere.*

Abdul punched the number again. Still, no answer. He made a mental note to remind Ishmael to check his phone battery, slipped into the shower in the bath room off his office, and began to sing as he prepared himself for the evening.

CHAPTER 9
Memories

Chelsey stared out the window. As she stared at the fields, already white, flying past, the landscape blurred till she felt somewhat dizzy. She wasn't sure if she was any better off heading east toward Anwar than she'd been locked up in Beirut. At least, she felt more comfortable around Michael Levine without Ishmael's foreboding presence. Nonetheless, Michael saddened her. He brought back too many memories of her mother. And, of course, her mother's memory triggered other sad memories, like the one of her best friends in high school, Marie.

Marie, it seemed, was everything Chelsey wasn't. She lived with both her parents, who neither divorced nor died, at least, not during high school. Always well but conservatively dressed, Marie played the oboe, while Chelsey was all thumbs with any musical instrument. And Marie was popular—both with teachers and students. She served as a student council member and helped organize homecomings, proms, ice-skating parties, group movie outings, and hayrides. In fact, the faculty and their class had voted her to attend Girls State, an honorary conference for the upwardly bound young woman. Chelsey found it odd that Marie paid her so much attention. She'd chide Chelsey into attending events. And Chelsey found it even odder than Marie considered Chelsey a close friend. "You're my bestest friend," she'd say, then run fingers through her own bobbed, raven hair. Suddenly, she'd squeeze one of Chelsey's hands. "So you've got to come to Homecoming."

"What could I wear?" Chelsey squeezed Marie's hand back but shook her head.

"Neil doesn't make all that much money. I don't feel right asking him for extras."

"Don't be silly. We can find you something. Sheila's not much bigger than you. We can use her dress from last year—Mom will help us take it in. I know she will."

"That's so sweet of you." Chelsey looked into Marie's eyes. Light blue and glistening, they were so full of energy, of light. Nonetheless, she slowly withdrew her hand. "But who would dance with me?"

"Oh, Chelsey." Marie rubbed one of Chelsey's shoulders. "You know Joey has a terrible crush on you. And Ben and Greg like you, too."

"Joey?" Chelsey gulped. "But he's so weird. He's scary." Marie had laughed. "No one says you have to dance with him. I'm just saying people like you—you just have to give them a chance."

No, Chelsey thought, she couldn't give them too much of chance. *Not getting close was safest. Always.* And even if Marie had coerced her into going to some of the student events, Chelsey kept her distance from everyone as much as possible. She was polite, yes. She tried to be kind, yes. But she wouldn't let herself feel too much. So even though Chelsey had no enemies then, she had few friends. And she'd shied away from running for student council or going out for sports—from anything outside the classroom that would allow others to evaluate her.

So she spent most of her high school years writing maudlin poetry or painting dark landscapes while other students went to parties, performed in school plays and concerts, or organized other activities. In fact, during those years, besides Neil, Marie was the only person for whom Chelsey felt friendship or any sort of trust. Other students scared her. But Marie was the closest to being a sister of anyone she'd known.

And that had resulted in another heartache. It happened just before graduation. In fact, it was after the Sunday tea for the Girls State reps and their mothers. Marie had coerced Chelsey into attending it, too. It'd been an April afternoon, after a rain, when the streets were still slick, but the sun had begun to poke through clouds. Marie's mother, Kris, had squinted when they went up the overpass. Suddenly, a semi had jackknifed across the left lane. Kris hit the brakes and the car swerved to the left. She let off the brakes and the car straightened. Then, coming from the other direction, a red Camaro swerved around the semi, sped up and slammed into the passenger's side where Marie sat. In the back seat behind the driver, Chelsey had sustained few injuries, but Kris had stayed in critical condition for a week. And Marie was DOA. Kris later learned the man who killed her daughter had been coked up and drunk and was running from the police. One day, about two months after the funeral, when Chelsey visited Kris, the mother shared another experience. After sharing tears and hugs, the two of them sat sipping tea on the porch of her bungalow that smelled of cinnamon and allspice.

"I would've rather it'd been me." Kris blew on her tea. "And you know, I was taken, too."

"You mean, outside your body?" Chelsey set down her cup.

"Yes. I went up, up into the skies, the clouds. Below, I saw my body bent over the steering wheel. But I wasn't in pain. And I didn't care to return. Up there, some tall, shimmery beings came toward me. They told me I had to go back—I needed to take care of Robin."

Chelsey picked up her cup again and sipped her tea. It was Red Zinger, one of her favorites. "And so, you did."

Kris nodded. "And I know—I know Marie lives on. I feel her with me. I feel her presence."

Afterwards, Marie's mother joined SADD and gave presentations to junior high students. She claimed this is why it happened, that Marie's death would help others save their lives. But Chelsey felt mainly pain—not much faith. And since the event, she'd become even more nervous about making close friends. Before the wreck, riding on freeways and highways always made her antsy. Afterwards, she had bordered becoming hysterical at the thought of driving them. Even when she drove to interviews in the suburbs, she avoided the fast routes whenever she could. Today, she had no choice, and certainly, her stare darted from the highway to the fields white to harvest back to the car's interior. But today, she was also worn-out. The lack of sleep the night before weighed upon her, and the heat gradually settled her into a heavy drowsiness, until finally, the highway's hum and the car's lulling rhythms sent her dozing.

CHAPTER 10
Hovering

Chelsey blinked and stretched her arms. With Scout on her lap, she was riding on a huge bus, but she didn't recall getting onto it. No one sat in the chair next to hers, but on the other side of the aisle, a white-haired man with a thick, gray mustache perched. He smacked his lips and blew a huge, pink bubble. Wearing a Yankees ball cap, a yellow-orange sweatshirt, and baggy jeans, he popped the bubble, laughed and whispered something to the woman beside him. The woman, wearing a felt fedora with a feather in it, giggled at his words. And her yellow curls—in a hairstyle akin to the blonde wig that Chelsey had donned earlier—bounced with her laughter.

Chelsey leaned back, then turned to survey the passengers riding in the long, white vehicle. She knew none of them. Most were older people like the ones across the aisle, but some of the men wore silk suits and wingtips. Some of the women were dressed in long, white gowns, while others wore jeans or polyester slacks. A number of them chatted with each other, but no one seemed to acknowledge her presence. In some seats, families sat, mothers with toddlers squirming or babies nursing, fathers holding young ones on their laps. She glanced over seat-after-seat of them, some decked out for a trip to Disneyland, others appearing to be *en route* to a wake. Then, in the last seat, she spotted two people who startled her. She blinked again. Yes, she was sure it was them: Marie and her mother sat together. They talked and laughed as if they were old friends. This confused her: She wondered when Marie would've met her mother and more than that, she wondered how they could have joined her on this bus.

She scanned the seats for Michael Levine—*had he put her on this bus? If so, where was he?* After searching each face, she couldn't find him. Apparently, he'd deposited her here and left. Perhaps the bus was headed for the embassy. She glanced out the window. But no fields blew in the wind as they had earlier. In fact, the bus seemed to hover above the ground because she could see nothing but clouds sliding across blue skies. The scenes from the windows looked more like scenes from an airplane than from a bus.

She looked behind her. A dark-haired, thin woman sat reading but glanced at Chelsey.

"Where are we going?" Chelsey asked and tried not to look as frightened as she felt.

The woman squinted and knit her eyebrows. "*Je ne comprend pas.*"

Chelsey hesitated a moment, then slowly spoke, taking care to inflect her final syllable. "*Ou allons nous?*" The woman shrugged and tilted her head to one side.

Finally, she spoke. "*Je ne sais pas. Ici ou la.*" She returned to her magazine.

This addled Chelsey. The woman didn't know where she was going—and yet, she was nonchalant about it. Chelsey wondered if they were riding a bus headed toward an asylum.

She looked back at her mother and Marie again. Yes, indeed, it was them. She put Scout in the seat next to hers and rose to walk back to them. She still didn't quite believe they were there, but as the minutes passed, the situation seemed more and more natural. Then, as she was making her way down the aisle, suddenly, she realized she'd forgotten a notebook containing some important paper, some document she needed to continue her journey, even though she still wasn't sure where this sojourn was headed. She remembered she'd left it at the last bus stop. So instead of moving back to her mother and Marie, she turned and grabbed Scout then moved toward the bus driver. She slipped into an empty seat behind him.

First, she waited and caught his eyes in the rear view mirror. "I must get off. I left my notebook." At first, she worried he didn't hear her, but within a few seconds, the ruddy-faced man smiled and nodded.

"I can get off here."

"Oh no. It's too far." He smiled again. "I'll take you back there." He promptly turned the bus around and headed the opposite direction. Now, Chelsey wasn't sure where the bus stop was located because she hadn't remembered stepping onto this bus. In fact, except for recalling she was missing something, something she left behind, she remembered nothing that had occurred between the time she rode in the cab with Michael Levine and she held Scout on this bus. But she knew she desperately needed that missing notebook. She couldn't remember what papers it contained or why she needed it, either.

The scenery outside hadn't changed—still clouds and sky with the sun breaking through here and there. Still, she could spot no fields, no trees, no highway. Perhaps, she considered, this was because of the angle of her seat. She wasn't sure how any of the situation made sense, but soon she accepted the surreal situation and watched the clouds on her trip back to the bus stop. Straight ahead, mirages appeared then disappeared as rapidly. After touring awhile, the driver pulled the bus over to a curb that somehow appeared while Chelsey hadn't been paying attention. He pulled back the lever that opened the doors, and clutching Scout at her chest, Chelsey disembarked. There was the stop, clearly marked. But she didn't see her notebook.

"It's inside the building," the bus driver said. "Go ahead. I'll return to pick you up once you have it."

Chelsey watched the bus zoom away, leaving behind a cloud of exhaust as white as those puffs in the sky. She stared after it a long while, until it became a speck on the horizon. Then, she turned to look at the building a block from the stop. Red-brick trimmed in gray, it had stretched about four stories high. *It looked like either a school or a prison*, Chelsey thought, and she felt uneasy about stepping inside. Nevertheless, she followed the concrete walk leading to its glass doors. Then, under the eave overhanging the doorway, she spotted her notebook, put Scout down, and together, they ran to pick it up. After flipping through it, she zipped it shut then shuffled back to the bus stop. Scout sniffed at bushes along the walk, relieved himself, and whined. She picked him up again.

Now, she worried the bus wouldn't come. So she carried Scout into the bench in the shelter, set him beside her and leaned back. It seemed like she'd closed her eyes but a few minutes when she heard a voice call her name.

It was Michael, softly calling her to get up. He'd found a place where they could eat. Chelsey pulled Scout of the carrier and secured his lease. "C'mon Boy!"

Michael crossed his arms. "You can't bring a dog into a restaurant."

"We aren't in New York." Chelsey frowned. "Besides, he hasn't eaten, either."

"So we'll bring him scraps from our table." Michael sighed and frowned, too.

"Look, I'm not walking into a restaurant with a dog in tow. Not even a lap dog."

"He isn't a lap dog."

"Whatever. Put him back in his cage."

"It's a carrier." Chelsey rubbed Scout's neck and whispered to the dog, "Who is he to make you starve outside? Your table manners are probably better than his." She glared at Michael. "Fine, if you won't let me take him in, you can bring me table scraps, too."

Michael turned and glanced at the restaurant. Even if it was built of solid, sand-colored stones, it was old, with large chunks of rock missing. The paint on its sign peeled, and some of the wood in the trim around the front window had begun to rot. The split wood frame obviously needed repairs. Maybe the owner wouldn't care if they brought in a dog. Perhaps he had goats feeding in the kitchen, who knows? On the other hand, even with this embarrassing situation getting the better of him, he was determined to cling to some dignity, some sense of civilization. He kept his arms crossed as he leaned back against the driver's window. "Look, if you like, I'll go see if they have scraps and we can feed the dog first. Would you come in without him then?"

Chelsey didn't answer at first but continued petting the dog. Michael wondered that with all the traveling and the no doubt, drug-tainted wine, if she hadn't felt much like eating. But now, it was, at least, well past noon, and he'd heard her stomach growl. She glanced at the restaurant and sighed. Michael figured she'd have to eat soon, and most likely, Scout was hungry.

Chelsey sighed. "Well, okay. But don't bring him chicken. The bones are dangerous. And bring a dish of water, too."

"Finally, some reason." Michael exhaled loudly, un-crossed his arms and followed the cab driver into the stone building. In a few minutes, he returned with lamb joints and scraps of pita bread piled high on a sheet of tin foil. Also he brought a Styrofoam cup filled with water.

"Oh no." Chelsey sighed. "I hate for him to drink from Styrofoam. He chews it and swallows it—bad for his digestion."

Michael glared at her. He said nothing as he dropped the food on the ground near the cab.

"Wait—we can pour it into his cup from his carrier." Chelsey smiled, let Scout out, and fiddled with the container. The dog grabbed a bone and drug it a few feet away, where he chewed on it with gusto.

Chelsey lifted Scout and the bone, then slid them into the carrier. She smoothed her jeans, stood and smiled. "Thank you."

Michael shook his head as he walked her to the building.

CHAPTER 11
Dèjá Vu

It was a shack, this place where the taxi driver had driven them. Some tables wobbled with uneven legs, and others were split through the middle, barely holding together. Frayed at their edges, the white ruffled curtains framing the smeared windows had faded through years of hanging in sunlight. Still, the owners had placed fresh flowers—some exotic breed—on each table, and smells of curry and nutmeg gave the place an exotic and friendly ambiance.

"You like falafel?" Michael flipped through a paper menu stained with grease and ghosts of red sauce. "There's couscous and humus, too. And I bet they have a Fatah salad with red beans, tahini, and yogurt."

"Yes. But I need meat." Chelsey looked at the menu. It was written in Arabic. She couldn't read a word. "You know Arabic?"

Michael grinned. "I know smells."

"Then why are you bothering with the menu?"

He grinned again. "I can read prices. Numbers are universal. You just need to know exchanges."

Chelsey frowned and crossed her arms. "I suppose that's why you had the cabby stop here."

"Don't take offense, Missy." Michael touched one of her arms. "I don't mean to be cheap. But we're lucky I'd hidden some money in my sock. Ishmael took my wallet. And we may be more hidden here."

"I didn't mean it that way." Chelsey smiled then shrugged. "Besides, it isn't like we're on a date. It was the word, 'exchanges.' Why are we here anyway?"

"Weren't you hungry?"

"No—not the restaurant. In this city. Why must we go to the embassy? We really must find Isadora."

"It's the safest place for us." Now Michael frowned, rubbed his chin, glanced at the cabby who sat alone sipping a soda at another table, then leaned close to Chelsey and whispered, "Look. I don't know who this Ishmael is—or who hired him. But it worries me. Isadora, at least, is safe. We aren't. We're Americans. And especially with your blonde wig, we stand out like peacocks at a crow convention."

"Peacocks at a crow convention?" Chelsey laughed. "How homey."

Michael seemed to blush, but the dim lighting obscured his coloring. "Now, Missy. How about lamb?"

Chelsey nodded. She didn't mind Mideastern food. In fact, in college back in Boulder, Colorado, she ate it often. She'd even prepared falafel and humus, albeit from mixes. But she quit buying falafel mixes when she discovered the crushed chickpea mixes were often nests for weevils. And the weevils didn't merely stay in the packages. They ventured out onto the kitchen counters, huddled under the toaster oven, and sometimes appeared in the living room. She'd thought they came out of the walls. Then someone told her about weevils—how the insects laid eggs in meal, often flour, but more often in ground legumes. So the only way she could rid her apartment of the rapidly growing bug metropolis was to throw away the package. She did and it worked.

Afterwards, she ate falafel only when out. And then, she'd wonder if she weren't eating cooked weevils within the patties. It didn't matter, she supposed. They'd be high in protein. Nonetheless, she'd lost much of her enthusiasm for the dish.

They were about halfway through the meal when they heard a car pull up outside. Michael flinched, wadded his napkin, and went to the window. Suddenly, he whirled around, rushed back to the table, threw a fifty on it, and grabbed Chelsey, still chewing lamb. She was so startled, she started choking.

"Oh no." Michael released his grip on her arm and gently pounded her back. "Not now. We must go."

Chelsey's eyes watered, her nostrils itched, and she couldn't breathe. She bent over and tried to sneeze or cough. Still rubbing her back, Michael put his other arm around her to inch her along to the back exit, or at least, to a hallway or a restroom in back where they could hide. Meanwhile, when Michael dropped the money on the table, the cabby rose from his seat. Perplexed, he moved in toward Michael.

"We need to get out," Michael said. "There's a guy after us. I don't know what he wants—but we can't let him find us here."

The cabby nodded. "Don't worry. You hide in back. I will deal with this man. Unless you are running from the police, eh?"

Michael smirked and shook his head. "Hardly." He shuttled Chelsey to the back hallway, where they found a storeroom and slipped inside. A mop fell out and nearly bonked Chelsey's forehead, but Michael caught it and drew it in with them as they huddled in the narrow storeroom. Now, Chelsey held her hands over her nose, pressing her fingers hard on the bridge of it. She felt the sneeze welling inside her— and she so desperately needed to sneeze. *But surely that would give them away.* Michael continued rubbing her back and listened to the men in the other room. They jabbered loudly in Arabic. Ishmael's booming voice sounded as if it were questioning the two others. At first, the restaurant owner started to answer. He said something, but the cabby interrupted him, sounding as if he contradicted him. The restaurant owner grew quiet, and Ishmael interrogated the cab driver.

Ishmael's voice grew louder. He sounded angry. But the poor little cabby remained steadfast, repeating the same response two, then three times. Someone kicked a wall or pounded a fist on a counter or table. The force of the blow shook the building so much, it reverberated even in the storage closet. Michael worried and listened for footsteps to move toward the back of the dining area. And now Chelsey's eyes watered so much, tears streaked her makeup, then rolled down her neck. She bent over again, and Michael tried to soothe her. But there was little he could do. Next, footsteps rang loudly across the creaky floor, and Michael stuck a finger inside a knot hole in the storage closet door and pulled it taunt. Finally, the front door slammed. A few seconds later, the car drove off. Michael shoved open the door.

"Ah-h-shu-u!" Chelsey breathed heavily. "I'm okay now." Still, she bent over again and exhaled.

Michael patted her back. "Thank God. I wasn't sure if you'd sneeze or choke to death trying not to. Let's see what the thug said to the cabby."

They ambled out of the hallway into the front room, where the owner and the cabby chatted in Arabic. The cabby seemed to be explaining something to the old man, but he quit when he saw Michael. The taxi driver nodded at the owner. "He knows this man after you— as a patron, not as a friend. He says the man works for Prince Abdul El Fashid. He's one of his henchmen, he says. And he asks why he was after you."

Michael shook his head and shrugged. "We don't know. He kidnapped us in New York—at the airport there, where I was to meet Ms. McKay for an interview."

The cabby squinted. "An American journalist?" The little man laughed. "Maybe the prince wants her to write a story about him and all his frolicking?" Then he stopped laughing, squinted again, and looked Michael over, scanning him from head to foot, staring especially at his hip pocket as if he looked for a gun. "But why would he want you?"

Michael shrugged again. "Who knows? Perhaps because I'm a fashion editor?"

The cabby laughed again. "That prince is a—how you say in America?—one snappy dresser. Maybe he wants a story in your magazine, too. Or maybe he wants to buy it."

Shaking his head, Michael responded, "What a strange way to get it. He should've just phoned me."

With Ishmael gone, the two sat back at their table. The owner offered to warm their food. In fact, once he glanced at the fifty dollars still lying by their plates, he said he'd cook them fresh meals, but Michael declined his offer.

Chelsey stared at the door a long time before she looked back at Michael. "I'd like to wrap that Ishmael in bacon and throw him in a pig sty," she said, then picked up a water glass and sipped from it.

Michael grinned. "I thought reporters were pacifists."

"I usually am. Guess that's relative." She sighed. "Besides, please don't try to psychoanalyze me or lump me in the bag with other journalists." She sighed again. "I'm a piece of abstract art no one's figured out yet." She smiled. "Not even me."

He stared at her a long minute before he paid the cabby fifty dollars for his help, finally asked his name, which was Ershad, and asked him to join their table. They dined slowly now, dipping the pita bread in humus and Chelsey carefully chewing the lamb. Even though it had grown slightly cold, the food tasted better now, mixed with the relief and peacefulness they felt after Ishmael's exit. So after they stretched and relieved themselves, the three of them piled back into the cab, and the driver swerved back onto the highway.

As they drove further east, Chelsey noticed the fields had grown even whiter, with heads of grain bending the stalks. The sky had remained clear, but ahead on the horizon, thunderheads were forming. She hoped they'd miss the storm. Even though she was more relaxed after eating, she still dreaded riding in the rain, especially on an unfamiliar highway. They wound along through the countryside and rounded a long curve that seemed to go on forever. Suddenly, just where the curve started to flow into a straightaway, a BMW blocked their lane. "Lord!" Michael said. "He's waited for us!"

"Who?"

"Ishmael."

"But it's not a limo."

Chelsey saw the BMW and Ishmael's swarthy face behind the wheel. She wanted to cry but didn't. Instead, she gasped.

"It's the car he drove to the restaurant," Michael said. "Go around it, Ershad."

No one stood near the car, no one sat in the driver's seat, and they could see no passengers. "Maybe he's broken down," Chelsey suggested.

As they swung around the BMW, they heard gun shots and the steering wheel whirled around, sending the cab to the left toward the shoulder. Ershad let off the accelerator and clutched the wheel, swinging the car back toward the road. "Blow out!" He managed to steer the now crippled cab around the BMW and back into the right lane. More gunshots came, but not at them. Ishmael continued to shoot at the cab's tires. The left rear one went, then the right. They were riding with just one full tire—the right front one. The car shimmied and wobbled as Ershad maneuvered it over the pavement, already bumping from the patching and resurfacing that made it resemble a patched pair of jeans. The car's bounces jolted Scout, who now stood on Chelsey's lap and barked loudly at the window. Still Ershad pressed the cab onward. Behind them, Ishmael scrambled up the hill, jumped in the BMW, and sped after them. Ershad shook his head. "We cannot outrun him."

"Pull over," Michael said. "There's nothing we can do." Once Scout smelled Ishmael, the dog stopped barking and started growling.

"It's okay, Boy." Chelsey scratched the spot between Scout's ears. "Well, no, it isn't. But settle down. That jerk might hurt you."

Michael shoved open the door, stepped out, and lumbered around the back of the cab to confront Ishmael who now marched across the pavement, his .45 in hand. "We give up." Michael nodded toward the gun. "So you can put that away."

Ishmael grinned broadly. He straightened his back and took his time slipping the gun into his shoulder harness. "I thought you would—how do you Americans say?—wise up." He strutted over to Michael as Chelsey forced Scout into the carrier, and swung her legs around to get out of the cab.

"H-ah!" Ishmael said. "The woman with her pet dog. But it helped me much. That's how I knew this pigeon was lying." He nodded at Ershad. "The dog had poked his head out of the window." He laughed again.

Chelsey looked at Michael and held his gaze. She bit her lip. "I knew we should've taken him inside."

Michael frowned. Nonetheless, he took her arm to help her out. He picked up their bags and the carrier and headed toward the BMW. Then he looked back at Ishmael. "You've got plenty of dough. Pay this man for his tires."

"What?" Ishmael raised his eyebrows. "He's lucky the prince doesn't—"

"Yeah?" Michael grinned. "And the prince might wonder why you had to recapture us, right?" Michael grinned again and held out a hand.

Ishmael dug in his pocket, pulled out a roll, and slipped off four hundred dollar bills. "That should do."

Michael grabbed the roll and pulled off another one hundred. He squinted. "Just in case he has to pay for towing."

Ishmael frowned and jammed the roll back into his pocket.

"Very well. But your lips better stay closed."

Michael smirked and said nothing as he paid Ershad the money and shoved the bags into the BMW's back seat.

CHAPTER 12
The Fourth Estate

No story had been this big in the small Nebraska city. At least, not for the past twenty-five years, not since the mayor's daughter eloped with a Broadway singer from New York. They'd fled to Paris to marry. Today, starting after Chelsey's phone call that came in a little after four p.m., Central Time, reporters bustled in and out of *The Globe*, trying to find someone who might know anything about terrorists in New York— or someone who knew someone who might know about New York kidnappers. And they were so frazzled, they duplicated efforts, each thinking he or she would succeed where the others had failed. Each of them called around the city, called state troopers, called the phone company to locate where Chelsey phoned from. But the office phone showed neither name of the caller nor the number on its digital screen. It was apparently blocked. And the telephone company told every reporter the same thing: that Chelsey and Jack weren't on the line long enough to trace the call. So after twenty minutes, Jack called a meeting with reporters and editors to brainstorm what to do next.

"It started with Leh, Lab—something like that." Jack scratched his head. "The connection was bad, lots of crackling and static, so probably she called from overseas." He wiped his nose with the back of a hand.

"Yeah," Russ, a new reporter, quipped, "or from Alabama."

Jack squinted and pulled his lips taut till he looked like a carved pumpkin shrunken from being left too long outside. "Right. Someone's abducted her from New York to take her to Alabama?" He flailed his arms and ambling with his usual limp, paced his office. With his limp, his white shirt hanging loose over his full belly, and his black slacks, he looked like a penguin waddling on an icy beach. "Imbeciles. I'm surrounded by them. "Look—someone—you, Russ—get on the Net and do a Google search for cities that start with Leh or Lab—"

The other five reporters left with Russ, each eager to find some lead to Chelsey's whereabouts. Greg, the managing editor, stayed behind. "I don't know what we can do right now, really—I mean, besides run the story." Greg's strongest attribute was his ability to remain objective. A bald-headed man with a gray goatee, he rarely became rattled, even during the hottest political races. Even during car crashes and murders, he maintained his aloof demeanor. In fact, when his wife was mugged in a supermarket parking lot, he remained calm. "We lost only forty dollars," he'd said the next day, "and Emily's just a bit shaken. She's okay." But today, even Greg kept shoving his hands deep into his pockets then pulling them out, then he'd sit on the edge of the chair one minute, then stand and move around the office the next. Finally, he pulled out a cigarette from Jack's case on his coffee table. Greg hadn't smoked in sixteen years. He tapped it on the table and cleared his throat. "If—or when—we discover where she called from, she might not still be there. And if she called from overseas, we can't get help from the FBI or the state patrol."

"There's the CIA." Jack lowered his voice and plopped into his chair. "A guy over there owes me favors. If he remembers me."

"So call him," Greg said, "if you think he can help." He settled on the edge of a chair next to Jack's desk, leaned over it, and whispered in his usual firm, level voice. "We need to use any resource you have, Jack. This could be an international incident. It likely is. It's got to be connected to Isadora's disappearance, you know it."

"Of course it is. But I need more info first." Jack bit his lower lip, slid open the narrow drawer running across his desk and fiddled with something inside it.

Russ stopped and stuck his head under the doorjamb. "If it's overseas, it might be the name of a country. Can't the GPS show that?"

"Whatever." Jack picked up his pipe and fished out the matches he'd fiddled for in his desk drawer. "Just get me some leads so when I call that guy I won't look like an idiot." He lit the pipe and puffed on it a few minutes. "And I want to know *pronto!* when you come up with something. And I mean anything!"

He inhaled the smoke from the pipe and plopped back in his chair. Chelsey was his best reporter, even if she hadn't been there the longest.

She was quicker, smarter than the others. She could get to the heart of a story, could see through the fluff. And it helped that she was a private eye. That occupation honed her perceptions and made her bolder than any reporter he'd known. Besides, she was a nice kid, not like most young reporters fresh out of J-school, not like those arrogant, self-obsessed hot shots who think the world owes them something. And with the Internet taking over all the large papers, they had to join community news forces. Most of them felt as if they were above that. Yes, he'd trade ten of those types for one like Chelsey.

But now, he regretted sending her on such a dangerous assignment. She was savvy, yes, but still awfully young. Of course, he hadn't realized it'd be that dangerous—and Levine had been there with her. But the thugs had snagged him, too—he'd heard that much during the call. And the story—this story was one he'd dreamed of—especially with its international possibilities. If what Greg said was true, this would put *The Globe* on the map. Yet now, the more he thought about that, the less he cared. Thirty-five years before, when he was a cub reporter, a young, arrogant jerk like the ones he found so annoying now, he'd have been as enthusiastic as Russ, he knew it. But today, such drama had lost its luster. Certainly, it wasn't worth anyone's life, especially of a young and bright kid like Chelsey. For the first time in at least twenty-five years, he truly worried about the precarious situation of one of his employees. And he wasn't sure what to do about it—or if he had the power to do anything. He glanced back at Greg then at the liquor cabinet. Jack hadn't taken a drink in five years, and at the moment, he wished his wife were there so he wouldn't be tempted to down a shot now.

For a few minutes, he fiddled with a pen, scribbled a few notes, tapped the pen on his desk, stopped, and tapped again. He rose from his desk, walked to the window across from it, stared out, and scanned the small city. Clouds festered on the horizon blocked the sun, except for rays that bled from behind them. This lighting cast elongated shadows across the city streets. He stared a few minutes more, stuck a match on his zipper, lit a cigar, then plopped back in his chair. *Shit*, he thought, Dee-Dee would be angry when he told her he'd have to leave town. He might as well let her get up her dander about this, too. He also felt guilty about putting Chelsey in danger. But then, the kid wanted to be a private eye. She didn't have any other addictions, but maybe Chelsey was an adrenaline junky and would have ended up in a life-threatening situation eventually anyway.

Glancing at the cabinet again, Jack pulled out a ring of keys. He sighed and tossed the keys to Greg. "Pour us a shot—at least three fingers—of the Glenmorangie. We need it."

CHAPTER 13
The Seventh Heaven

After testing more DNA samples, Dardiel and Liwet had decided that Michael must not have been on Emeth's list after all. Apparently, some typo had slipped through, and his name had been added to the others. Of course, most likely, two Michael Levines walked the earth, and perhaps Gabriel had been following the wrong one. Or perhaps, Michael was not to be brought with Ms. Chelsey McKay. Before acting further, they knew they must bring up this discrepancy with their leader so they set an appointment with Emeth's secretary to discuss the matter, then they went about their business of converting the laboratory into a ship that would run at least a thousand times faster than the speed of light. It would not be an easy endeavor.

They had to rebuild and expand the mirror screens. This construction would allow the passengers to observe the action on their native planet as they rose into the heavens. And simultaneously, the mirror screens would prohibit beings on the earth and other planets they would pass during their journey from seeing inside the cruiser. Outsiders would see merely their reflections. Emeth had stressed how crucial this device would be as a way to gain the earthlings' loyalty. But such a construction required much work. This meant huge areas of mirrored glass must replace the gleaming, brushed synthetic steel, which other Serkerpians had to remove and reconstruct into other vehicles. So today, Lewit and Dardiel measured the huge, high walls. They fluttered up and down with tape measures, then calculated the size the replacement mirrors must be to fit exactly into the ship.

"I hope we are staying on schedule." Liwet's brow furrowed as he pressed the measure against the ceiling's edge. "Has Gabriel sent any news about the other passengers? Have they been assembled yet?"

Dardiel shook his head. "You're always so concerned about time, my friend. You know we work in the dimension where Time is always correct, *always* on schedule. Why do you continue to fret so?"

"It appears so much is left to be done." He fluttered his wings and continued hovering in place. "And I do wish we could travel with Gabriel and meet the passengers before it is time to collect them. Obviously, there is no time for that."

"Talking about Time again." Dardiel shook his head. Running fingers along the measure, he dropped down fifty feet, marked it, then slid the tape in between his fingers, and followed it downward to the floor. "Besides, that is not part of our appointment. We must concern ourselves solely with our duties. Remember what happened during the revolution? Too much questioning. See, you must admit, in many ways, our positions are more peaceful. We need not interact with the *homo-*

sapiens—the earthlings—until after they've graduated. Poor Gabriel must deal with the doubters, the naysayers. That is the most difficult task. Sometimes those earthlings must become blind to truly see. Take that fellow, Saul, for instance. How awful. And then, keeping him on track still took some doing—from all of us, you remember? Too often, he came across as a misogynist." He marked the tape at the floor's edge. "Marked it. You can come down now."

"I also do not understand why some of these people are on the list." Liwet brought his wings together behind his back. "Their records show they are not all church-goers. Some of them, like the American reporter, do not even confess their beliefs. This is highly irregular. It does not follow the guide book."

Dardiel fluttered his wings and perched his hands on his sides. "The book says all things are possible. And Emeth sees through to the hearts of the earthlings. We cannot see them that completely. We are able to perceive merely their external actions. He sees the *true* motives behind those actions and words. Who are we to question him?" He finished jotting down numbers, calculated them, and then double-checked his figures on one of the computers lining the laboratory's convex walls.

"But that one hides her heart. She refuses to share it."

"Emeth sees through to it. She still nurses a wound there. Can you truly blame her? Besides, she shares it with her animal friend, another species."

"No. I neither blame her nor condemn her." Liwet wrinkled the area where a nose rests on a *homo sapien* face. "I am just searching for the logic, the rationale behind this list."

Dardiel laughed. "At times, Liwet, you sound so much like an earthling. Ah, *logos*. Once, earthlings longed to know the true *logos*. The truth. Now, for more than a thousand years, logic has become merely a human tool, or more accurately, a *homo sapien* game. The *homo sapiens* twist it and warp it to fit their beliefs. They aver they use 'reason' to support the most preposterous notions, including war and infanticide. Think of that madman called Hitler. He bolstered his atrocities with logic—more accurately, rhetoric—with false notions of a superior 'race,' supported with slanted, purportedly 'scientific' studies. And it hasn't stopped. Take, for instance, those earthlings who rant about animal rights. Have you noticed how many of them believe it is perfectly reasonable to slaughter their own young—merely because they reside inside wombs? Sometimes, they hire physicians to kill those infants, who, a day later, would have been born naturally, and then, any person killing the babies would be prosecuted. They construct syllogisms with ludicrous premises then use them to support preposterous theorems, whether they be true or not. For example, they might say, 'All blue beings are dogs. George is blue. Thus, George is a dog.' Whereas, in truth, George is a chimpanzee. All such theorizing, hypothesizing in logic's name! I doubt if even ten percent of earthlings know or understand the true origin of *logos*. And those who do often use it to manipulate other earthlings for money or power or both."

"Goodness." Liwet's eye sockets widened and his eyebrows flickered. "You sound as if you detest the species."

"No. I do not." Dardiel sighed. "But moreover, they frustrate me. So many of them chase after what they deem to be love, yet it is not *agape*, or even *philia*, but it is merely *eros*. And they do it so often in reckless disregard of any sort of reason, yet they refuse to give love. Or they sacrifice for some media image of 'courtly' love and expect immediate compensation—immediate gratification. They do not realize love is a commitment, not a feeling. And so many of them close off their hearts, even more than Ms. McKay. No, my friend, I do not detest them. I worry about them the way they worry about other species with lesser brain capacity. Have you not gleaned the same propensities in the earthling *homo sapiens*?"

"Of course, I have." Liwet smiled. "How could I mention them to you when you chide me so often for my impatience? You would merely attribute my observations to my most apparent character flaw."

Dardiel chuckled. "*Touché*, my friend. You have shown me I, too, suffer from impatience. Perhaps secretly, I also fret about Time. We know what is coming in the future—even if we will not know the time until the perfect hour has arrived. And I worry these earthlings will not understand—and save more of their species—before it is too late."

Liwet wrinkled his brow again. "How much longer do they have to apply to join the list—or to change their ways so Emeth will add them to it?"

Dardiel shook his head. "I do not know, my friend. Only Emeth knows. He has been adding more names lately—names that surprise me, too. And yet, who am I to understand the reasoning? Emeth alone experiences absolute knowledge. No, I do not know the cut-off date—any more than I know the date we depart from this universe to return home. It is bet this way. We work. We follow the plan. All will happen in the time it is meant to happen."

CHAPTER 14
Michael Remembers

Again, Chelsey and Michael were at Ishmael's mercy. At least, this time, Michael had something to hold over him, even if it was extortion. He didn't like that game, but he did like the advantage it gave him. *The control. And control was crucial, not just now—but always.* Otherwise, his world would merely dry up and wither away, become small, narrow, and pinched. He refused to live in a narrow, pinched box that other people could kick around. As a Jewish boy growing up in Brooklyn, he'd learned that to succeed he needed to be kind to people, upbeat. But also, he had to let their negatively, their manipulations, and their treacheries just bounce off him. Until finally, he'd stand up to them, but only after he had them snagged in their own nets. Ishmael was typical, like so many of the publishers he'd dealt with—pushy, imperative personalities. And Michael would let them push him to a point until he earned his keep, till he'd gained control. Like today. Then he'd make his move. Now, he watched the telephone poles flashing by, marveled how they looked like crosses across this empty plain. He also wondered what would happen next. They'd see Prince El Fashid, yes. *What did the spoiled prince want with them anyway?* He already possessed the cool Isadora Winger for whatever reason. *Was he planning to add her to his harem?* Michael couldn't figure out why the prince wanted Chelsey and him in his palace. He also wondered how he might put the prince in a stronghold as he had Ishmael.

He glanced at Chelsey, who held her dog in her lap, and together, they stared out the opposite window. He reached over and rubbed one of her arms. She glanced back at him, smiled, then turned back to stare at the landscape whizzing by. She'd certainly grown up. Yes, in some ways, she resembled Penny, but unlike her mother, Chelsey seemed to keep her passion in check. Or perhaps, she lavished it on her dog. He chuckled to himself at the thought of bringing a dog on a business trip. Now, that might be something her mother would have done.

He leaned back in the seat and thought about Chelsey's mother. Penny had been a sexy woman, a passionate one to be sure. And talented—the woman could paint, design lay-outs, and was a whiz with computer graphics. Had he loved her? He once thought so—but he was so young, then, less than Chelsey's age today. Yes, he'd been attracted to Chelsey's mother, Penny. *But love?* The truth was, Michael Levine wasn't sure he'd ever truly known love, except perhaps with Isadora. That friendship had started more than ten years ago. And indeed, their love was more of a friendship than a romance. He and Isadora lived together sometimes, when it was convenient, for maybe a month or two. But more often, they lived separate lives. Michael never felt jealous of

Isadora's flings—not like he had with Penny's. It sickened him when Penny had married Hank, a worthless druggy who beat her, Michael was sure. And he'd never met Jules, the man responsible for her murder. Jules hadn't killed Penny, but his army buddy did. And together they ran off until the police arrested them. Jules got off, but Michael's instinct had told him he should get her away from Jules—long before the murder. In fact, he still could not forgive himself for not opening his small studio to Penny and her daughter. He hadn't lied to Chelsey—he'd wanted to bring Penny and Chelsey to live with him in New York—partially to keep her away from the jerks that clung to her. But back then, he didn't have the money to do it, and he feared if he tried, she'd end up back with Hank anyway. God, Michael realized he was so young then—such a pup.

Probably his failure then made him more protective of Chelsey today. He cared for her ardently, as if she were a daughter or a niece. He wished he'd watched her grow up. *Mais c'est la vie, c'est domage*, he nearly said aloud. He thought again about Paris, about strolling with Penny over cobblestones there in the rain. She'd worn platform boots, she always did. She said they made her taller so she looked slimmer. They also made her wobble when they were walking over the cobblestones.

She'd slipped, and he remembered how soft her cheeks were when they fell against his. He could smell her sweet perfume again. And he recalled sitting on the bridge with her, watching the Seine. He'd stuffed a croissant into her mouth. She'd laughed and chided him about trying to make her fat, her light blue eyes glimmering, the sunlight reflecting off her blonde curls, making them look almost like a halo encircling her. Suddenly, he inhaled deeply and stopped his reverie. Then he sighed and glanced at Chelsey again. Yes, she had her mother's eyes—clear and direct. Sincere. Unlike most of the women in the Apple. "What are you thinking?" he asked.

Chelsey looked back at him. Her eyes were watery. "Not much. Only wondering." She smiled weakly. "I guess we should just enjoy the trip. And that was a good move there." She tilted her head toward Ishmael. "Maybe he won't bully us so much now, even if we're still his captives." She tugged at her wig. "Guess this disguise didn't help much." She tore off the hairpiece and shook her head. "And it makes my head itch."

Michael grinned and shrugged. "Perhaps the prince will put us up in his palace, treat us like guests. You never know."

"Yes, he will likely do so." Chelsey crossed her arms. "But this is just insane. Obviously the prince doesn't want us in New York. Why?" She leaned back and closed her eyes. "I wonder if he has terrorist groups there planning another attack on the city? But the Saudis are our allies. Perhaps Jack's discovered something connected with the prince and Ishmael. Probably he'll send someone to rescue us."

"You contacted Jack?"

"I thought I told you. I phoned him just before you arrived. But the line crackled so much, I'm not sure what he heard. I think he knows we've been kidnapped. The call cut out when I'd just started to tell him where."

"Good girl." Michael squeezed one of her knees and chuckled. "Jack will figure it out. It might take him awhile, but he'll get it. And we have old buddies in the CIA."

"You do?" Chelsey's eyes lit. "He never told me that." It bothered Chelsey that she'd failed to draw that piece of information from Jack. She began to doubt her ability as a private eye. Certainly, she should have gleaned that. But Jack had never alluded to those connections.

"We haven't talked to those guys in thirty years." Michael's eyes seemed to focus on a distant space.

At least, knowing that Jack hadn't contacted his CIA buddies since before she was born made her feel a little bit more confident about her abilities. She drew a hand to her lips. "Say—do you think you could locate anyone around here?"

"Fat chance now." Michael grinned then leaned back in the seat. "Why do you think we were headed for the embassy? Who did you think I was sending for Isadora?"

Chelsey shrugged. "I dunno. Ambassadors, maybe?"

Michael shook his head. "I need time to think about this one."

He sprang from the chair, then sat again. "We need sleep."

"You might be right." Chelsey settled back in her seat, closed her eyes, and cuddled with Scout, but try as she might, she couldn't yet relax. It was as if she were bracing herself for the drive back to Beirut. "I still haven't deduced why the prince would want the two of us there. Even if you knew about Isadora, the prince wouldn't need you in the palace. He could've sent Ishmael or one of his other lackeys to bribe you—or even kill you. And who could have told him I was doing a story on you—and investigating Isadora's disappearance? Only Jack and one other person at *The Globe* knew. You didn't tell anyone, did you?"

Michael shook his head. "I don't know how he discovered that. Jack and I kept it on the QT." Then he shrugged. "It could be the prince doesn't know about your investigation. Unless Isadora figured it out and told him."

Chelsey sighed. "I'd considered that. But after you told me she was happy, it wouldn't make sense that she'd worry the prince about a possible investigation. Besides, she told you where she was."

"I didn't mention you to Isadora." Michael looked at the road ahead. A mirage formed on the horizon. It was blue and shimmery. And what looked like hazy palm trees bent over the glistening water. It continued shimmering awhile, emulating a welcome oasis across the hot desert highway. It disappeared. But he noted it had looked as real as any oasis he'd ever seen.

CHAPTER 15
The Prince Goes a Courting

After Prince Abdul El Fashid left the office, he felt even more energetic. In fact, he'd become hyper. He refused to take a cab or have his chauffeur escort him home. Tonight, he was determined to shop awhile, to wander through the streets, smell the curry and allspice wafting from cafes, as if he were just another man, a commoner, and he would take time to truly *see* the colors and splendid, flowing robes, perhaps even red bandanas, on city passersby to help him think a bit and perhaps, figure out a precise plan to win over the American woman he was anxious to meet. Perhaps she was the one who could fill the hole inside him—the emptiness that all the fast cars and jets in the world could not appease. Or perhaps, this was another empty dream, another fantasy. Nevertheless, the fresh air would be good, he assured himself, and he followed a sidewalk toward a market area. Yes, he order orchid arrangements for their table, but he wondered if he should buy a corsage to pin on her wrist. Then again, perhaps she would be offended by this overture. Already, she was likely dismayed by being held up from her mission—to help Michael Levine rescue Isadora. *Ha! As if Isadora needed such assistance.* Such a publicity stunt.

When Abdul offered Isadora $500,000 to stay at one of his palaces and join the otherworldly beings on a pilgrimage, she had eagerly accepted. Perhaps she had not told her American friends these details. And why Chelsey cared so much about Isadora's welfare, the prince could not fathom, but he knew she must be a compassionate woman. He was almost sorry he had to stop her from seeing the Goddess. But it was crucial Chelsey did not interfere with the plan. Besides, he had booked Chelsey in one of the city's finest hotels, and surely, Ishmael saw to it that she received exquisite treatment. So perhaps, a wrist corsage would be a nice finishing touch. Finally, after debating the idea another ten minutes, he darted into a flower shop, found a gardenia and ordered the keeper to add a sprig of ivy with tendrils and fashion it into a wrist design, then headed back into the street with this small package.

While he imagined what the American woman looked like, he strutted down the sidewalk, occasionally gazed at sunlight reflecting off clay rooftops, and watched thin wisps of clouds sift through the sky. Now and again, he glanced at the bay. Yes, sometime, when the time was ripe, they would dine together on a rooftop. Naji, his butler, would cater to them, the two of them sitting at a table under a sliver of a moon, only stars and candles lighting their faces. Or perhaps, they could find a private spot along the beach and one sunny afternoon, set up a picnic. He imagined each scene in detail, the exotic smells of the food, her face and her perfume, and became so engrossed in his thoughts that he nearly stumbled over an old woman ambling ahead of him. Wearing a blue hijab and a long, burka-like gown, she carried a large tote bag filled with her day's purchase of groceries. The prince turned, his elbow hit the woman's bag and sent two pomegranates tumbling onto the sidewalk. One of them rolled toward the curb and the street.

"Sorry! So sorry! I'll get them!" he said and scrambled after the spinning fruit. Inside his head, his father's voice chided him. "Don't go on the street alone," just as his father, the king had warned him over and over, "always take a footman." Now Abdul understood why, and the voice confirmed what an imbecile he had been. Certainly, a prince squandered his dignity when he stumbled after fruit rolling into the street. But another voice in the prince's head argued back that really, he dressed in western clothes, always he did—so no one here knew his position. He looked just like another businessman, albeit a clumsy one, meandering home from work.

While the war continued inside his head and he hurried after one obstinate pomegranate that rolled further into the middle of the road, a taxi whirled around the corner and headed closer and closer to the prince. The driver hadn't seen him at first, then finally, he braked. Shocked, the prince froze and stared at the car before he thought to back up to the curb. The cab's elongated shadow fell over him as the bumper rolled nearer and nearer. The tires screeched and did not seem like they would stop. A whirlwind of scenes from his life, from his boyhood in

Riyadh, where he ran up and played upon huge sand dunes, sifted through his head. But finally, the tires caught hold, merely inches away. Then, from the abrupt stop, muddy water splashed onto his white suit, streaking the lapels and dappling the entire side of his pants with large, thick drops. A dirty mist sprayed his mustache and dribbled down around his chin. "Idiot! Out of the street!" the cabby yelled. Dazed, the prince could manage no more than to stand there. Meanwhile, a crowd had gathered at the curb, and many people laughed.

The driver still cursed him as he backed up, then whisked around the prince, shooting more mud. Finally, Abdul shook the heaviest bits of the brackish mud off his arms, ambled back to the woman, and dropped the fruits in her bag. He looked down at his suit and shook his arms again. The woman thanked him but hobbled away. Passersby stared and kept their distance as they chuckled, their laugher echoing behind them. He sighed and looked back at the street.

There the wrist corsage lay smashed in mud. *So much for romance.* Plus, now, his hair was filthy and he had but an hour now to dress, return to the office, shower again and again dress for dinner. *Living like a commoner had its drawbacks*, he thought as he pulled his cell phone out of his jacket and called his chauffeur. He was unsure if he could ever escape this world his father had built and step into this one that it seemed even the simplest man could handle. But it seemed this day had shown him he lacked that simple skill. Perhaps, it was not his destiny to escape his father's world. Crestfallen, he glanced once more at the flower shop. He still wanted to buy the American a corsage, but he looked so disheveled that he decided to save the corsage for another day.

And now as he shuffled back to his office, the news of the world weighed heavy on him. While he was leaving the office, Ms. Dune mentioned that today, some rebels had bombed three U.S. fast food restaurants in the city. He was so wrapped in his fantasies then, he had not paid much attention to her words. Now they haunted him. In fact, he wondered if the Americans Ishmael held knew about this unrest against their country. Would they hate him? And then, another, even more terrible thought struck him. He had not heard from Ishmael, and the prince now worried about the Americans. *Had the three of them been in one of those restaurants?* He picked up his pace and tried calling Ishmael again.

CHAPTER 16
Back in the States

Just after opening the bottle, Jack had ordered Russ to call an associate editor in Lebanon, Tennessee, just in case this kidnapping was merely domestic. Plus, he thought it wouldn't hurt to check to if any terrorist activity had erupted there. Then, the AP news came in and reported the Lebanon bombings. Jack stood by the machine, awestruck. U.S. fast food restaurants in Beirut, Lebanon? What was behind that? Anti-American demonstrators again? Then, it dawned upon him— Chelsey had called from Lebanon, but obviously not the city in Tennessee. No wonder the phone connection was so bad. *Yet who would kidnap Chelsey and Michael and cart them across the ocean?* Fundamental terrorists? Were terrorists abducting Americans from our shores now? Was this just a random kidnapping of random citizens? Surely no one was trying to traffic Chelsey, and certainly not Michael. Had the abduction something to do with Michael's heritage? Had Chelsey and Michael merely been in the wrong place at the wrong time?

Yes, Greg had been right—this was international business. This was big time. Jack ordered his secretary to make reservations on a plane bound to the country. It was time he left the office and ventured back into reporting. He ripped off the sheet and took it back to his office, where he filled the shot glasses again. He opened the door and called for Greg, who shuffled back.

"Have another." Jack cleared his throat then grinned. "You're in charge, now. Run the head about Chelsey's abduction." He downed the shot. "Me, I'm on the road again."

Greg blinked then drew together his eyebrows. "What? You're leaving town? Now?"

Jack shoved the other glass toward Greg. "Going to Lebanon, my friend. And not the one in Tennessee. You see what just came in from overseas?"

"No—I was in the back with the computers and—"

"Take a look at this." Jack handed Greg the sheet. "Our girl isn't in Tennessee. I didn't think she was, but the thought of her being kidnapped and taken overseas was too dramatic."

Greg read the release. "You're kidding. But why do you think that's where—"

"Obviously, terrorists are getting antsy again," Jack snapped. "And they've probably got some anti-American factions in the Apple. That'd be why they'd take her—and Levine, a Jew—to Lebanon. But not Tennessee. Tennessee never seemed right. I just thought no one would take her out of the country." Jack had felt a little stupid about asking his staff to check out Lebanon, Tennessee. On the other hand, he'd wanted to cover every possibility. "Run another copy of that release, too. Can probably pick it up on the Net." Jack grabbed the sheet. "I'm taking this one with me. And have Russ run me a search on Beirut, Anwar, Tripoli. Get anything he can on terrorist groups—names of leaders, political goals, where they hole up, everything." He plopped into his chair and nodded at the remaining shot. "And drink up. We've got work to do. Now, I've got to call my friend to get the real scoop."

Greg downed the shot and hurried to the press room. Jack watched him close the door before he pressed any buttons. He hadn't wanted to mention it to Greg, but now, he worried that Chelsey might have been in one of the restaurants. The release only mentioned the bombings— nothing about hostages. But who knows? Just the headline had been released. His CIA friend was stationed in Iraq. He wondered if he'd be able to meet him in Anwar or Beirut, take him on a tour of Beirut's underground scene. Then, another thought haunted him: *How would he present this plan to Dee-Dee?* He'd promised her no more out-of-town trips, except to press conventions that she attended with hm. And he'd stuck to his vow for ten years. She'd be irked. Irked? She'd be rabid. She'd scream and scream about his lack of attention, his workaholism. It'd be awful. And he hoped she wouldn't threaten to divorce him again. He hated it when she did that. After all, they were in their sixties. In the past twenty-five years, she'd learned to put up with his eccentricities— his pipe smoke, his sometimes sleeping in his clothes when he'd drag in at four a.m. on election nights or when a computer glitch held up production. The thought of a divorce rattled him. He wasn't up to such nonsense. And there was no getting out of this trip. He'd gotten his star reporter into this jam—he had to be there to help her out. He poured another shot and lit his pipe before he called the agent. He figured he'd probably need another one, too, before he called his wife. He downed the shot and pressed the buttons on the phone.

CHAPTER 17
On the Road back to Beirut

Chelsey dozed awhile, and for a change, she didn't dream. Then, she blinked herself awake, and started watching the winding highway. Just ahead of them was a Ford, a Silver Escape, probably about five years old. Ishmael had slowed down and now tailgated the SUV, which was going no faster than sixty-five, maybe seventy at the most. He was frowning and kept edging so close to the bumper, it made her nervous.

They were so close, that even from the back seat, she could read on the car's right rear, above the bumper, a funny little outline of a fish with "Jesus Lives" squished inside it. Back home, she'd seen those emblems before, sometimes without writing and sometimes with Greek letters inside the outline. She'd also seen the Darwin creature with legs sprouting. But she thought it odd to see such a sign in this Islamic country. She stared at it awhile to keep her mind off of Ishmael's driving. The sunlight made it glisten and after she'd looked at it a few minutes, it started to repeat itself, like hallucinations or mirages on the highway. Finally, they came to a straight-away, and Ishmael swerved around the vehicle. But a ghost of the fish's outline still shimmered in the air.

"Are you okay?" Michael asked, his voice softer now.

"Oh, fine." She forced a smile. "I mean, as much as possible."

"You seem to sleep a lot."

"Just when I'm riding. Plus, the day before yesterday, before we took that plane, Ishmael drugged my wine. I still don't know with what. Since then, except for worrying, I haven't had much energy."

"You aren't pregnant?"

Chelsey laughed. "Hardly."

"You're sure?" He winked.

"Quite." She smiled. "That'd be impossible. Entirely." Then she remembered it was about time for her period. Perhaps that's why she'd been so drowsy. She sighed when she realized she hadn't packed any pads. *It figured.* Always when she travelled, too. While she'd frantically prepared for the New York trip, pressing suits, folding jeans and shirts, stuffing in underwear and panty hose, and toiletries, she hadn't thought about the time of month. Of course, had they been in the states, that wouldn't be a problem. Now, here, in this strange situation, she wondered what to do—no way would Ishmael allow her to dash into a drugstore alone. Okay, then, he'd have to just follow her into a store. Just picturing the scene of him and Michael escorting her to the feminine hygiene aisle embarrassed her. Afterwards, they'd be hovering around her at the check-out counter. And now, what was worse, she'd have to keep checking each time she went to the john to make sure nothing would spot her clothes. At least, this morning she'd switched to jeans. No more panty hose with persnickety crotches and constant runs while she was on this strange excursion.

She glanced back at Michael. "Do you have children?"

"Not that I know of." He grinned. "Let's say, not officially."

She frowned and wondered why men had to allude to their virility for their self-esteem. Odd, she thought, that a man Michael's age would still be so insecure about it.

"Did you ever marry?"

Michael shook his head. "Haven't found the right one. And you, Missy?"

"Of course not." She leaned back and pulled the dog closer to her then looked back at him and grinned. "I'm too young."

"Yeah, me, too."

Chelsey said nothing but rubbed Scout's head and looked back at the white fields. She'd hoped Michael would've been married. Then, she might not feel as awkward buying pads in front of him. She wondered, too, why he hadn't and if he'd truly loved her mother. She considered that perhaps he hadn't gotten over her mother's death. Perhaps after that tragedy, like Chelsey, Michael had feared becoming too close to anyone. But she wasn't sure. So then, she looked back at him. "If you don't mind me imposing, just how close are you to Isadora?"

"Hey—you're the press." He smiled, this time, a crooked smile without teeth. "It's your job to impose. Besides, people know Isadora and I've lived together off and on. But mainly, we're close friends."

"So what's the deal with the prince? Why didn't he just ask her to stay with him? Did she sound like she'd been abducted?"

"Not really." He wrinkled his brow. "It's strange, though. Not so much her being with the prince. But she spoke about some journey they've planned. I don't understand it completely. Too much is still fuzzy. She was vague about where they're going. And she didn't want the press to know her whereabouts. But with all the trouble we've had with the Mideast, and with so many papers running the story about Isadora's disappearance, I thought I'd better help you check out things. I'd hate to see the feds get involved with this—and have it just be some romantic fling or spat or whatever. That'd be a waste of resources. And taxpayer monies have been wasted far too much for far too long. If you and I put our investigative talents together, we should be able to unearth what's happening here."

"You mean, you *planned* to come to Lebanon?" Chelsey sat up in the seat, shoved Scout aside, and crossed her arms. "Wish you'd have told Jack so. I mean, I wasn't expecting to take this trip. I was uneasy enough traveling alone to the Apple."

"Hey—simmer down. I wasn't expecting you to, either. I wasn't sure if I'd come all the way to Lebanon. In fact, I wasn't sure just how to investigate the disappearance without creating a ruckus." He smirked. "Now, here we are, ruckus and all. Sorry about that."

She sighed. "I'm surprised you wanted to 'investigate' this yourself. Why didn't you hire a private eye?"

"Isadora's welfare remains important to me, even if we are no longer together." Michael shrugged. "A private eye wouldn't care as much about her as I do."

"Yeah, I get it." Chelsey's arms relaxed. Although Michael's comment tempted her, she didn't tell him about her free-lance job. She figured he'd continue to be more forthright, more fatherly, if he remained unaware of it. So she looked out the window and watched the rough landscape fly by. After a while, she felt nauseous. She glanced at Ishmael, then rubbed her waistline and looked at Michael. "I wish he'd slow down. His swerving and weaving has been making me queasy."

"Hey! Up there! Slow it down!"

Ishmael grunted.

"I mean it!" Michael cleared his throat. "She's getting sick."

Immediately, Ishmael let up on the accelerator. They rode without further incident back to Beirut.

CHAPTER 18
Fatima Seeks the Prince

Moving stealthily, as if she were a cat stalking its prey, Fatima wove through the Hotel Portemilio's lobby. There, numerous businessmen in gray summer suits, tourists in jeans and bright yellow and red Hawaiian or T-shirts, and a few locals milled around the elevators. She'd spent a couple of evenings here before—one for business, one for pleasure. But she wasn't attuned to the building's lay-out, and she'd never met the prince. She'd seen no portraits of him, either, merely newspaper shots taken from a distance. Not being able to spot him immediately made her more nervous. So she tapped her ruby-colored nails on her purse, and then and again, drew a hand to her cheek as she squeezed through the crowd and followed signs to the restaurant, where she glanced around to locate the *maitre d'*. Then she spotted him, she was sure. She could tell by his tux and his confident stance, he was likely the man. He clutched a glass of sherry while he talked to a bartender. Immediately, she strode over to him.

"Where is Prince El Fashid's booth?" She sighed, then mustered up the breathiest voice she could conjure and still remain audible.

The *maitre d'* scanned her, looking first at her stiletto sling-backs, then his gaze moved to her ankles, her off-black hose, then to her silky skirt so delicate that with the sun behind her, it looked so transparent, she looked almost nude, and finally to her low-cut, lacy black blouse. "You are here for the prince?"

She nodded. The *maitre d'* squinted and cleared his throat. Fatima knew he didn't believe her.

"Ishmael el-Haddid arranged a meeting between him and me."

At the mention of Ishmael's name, he lifted his chin then turned and motioned for a host to join them. After making a mental note to contact the prince, he decided to take no chances. He pointed out a curtained booth to the host, not visible from the prince's usual table, and the man seated Fatima in that place in the corner.

She slid her thighs and plump derriere across the smooth wood bench. The booth and table were elegant, certainly, more luxurious than any setting where she'd eaten. But the curtains blocked her view so she wouldn't be able to see the prince approach. Perhaps that wouldn't matter, she considered. If this was his booth, surely he'd arrive here soon. Ishmael had said eight o'clock. It was now 7:58. She ordered wine, set her purse beside her, and thumbed through the menu. Too bad she wouldn't be having dinner with him. At times like these, she cringed with a bit of self-pity. Why had she been born into a narrow life that left her no choice but to be a working woman to obtain even the smallest luxury? *How nice to be born a royal, to live in this world of finery.* She also thought it odd that Ishmael had hired her to occupy the prince for merely an hour. On the other hand, Ishmael was strange and often gave her unusual assignments. But he paid quite well—and promptly. She ran a finger over the menu, felt its satin ridges. Such luxury. A least, with her occupation, she savored a taste of it here and there.

Shortly thereafter, the prince arrived and the *maitre d'* greeted him. "A woman said she was to meet you here, Your Highness."

"The American?" Prince Abdul's heart raced. "She came alone?" Had the reporter been so brave that she came to see him by herself? Perhaps this girl was ready for romance, too. His chest swelled and his eyes became darker, more intense.

The *maitre d'* shook his head. "No. This woman is not an American."

"Hmmm?" The prince's chest fell. He rubbed his nose, then twisted one end of his mustache. "And she says she's here to see me?"

The *maitre d'* nodded. "She said Ishmael set up an appointment with her."

The prince knit his eyebrows and frowned. "Ishmael? There must be some mistake. Ishmael is to escort the American woman and the American man to my table."

"Should I send her away, Your Highness?"

The prince knit his eyebrows again. He didn't speak for a minute, then he said. "No. I will talk with Ishmael first. There is some mistake, some misunderstanding. But she is innocent and should not be shamed for it. Let her drink wine and bring her some appetizers. Put it on my bill."

With that, the *maitre d'* escorted the prince to the booth hiding his reserved table, even more luxurious than the one where Fatima sat, then ordered a waiter to attend to Fatima.

Meanwhile, the prince punched out Ishmael's number once more, but he was so excited to find they were about to arrive, he forgot to ask Ishmael about the woman sitting in a booth not far from his own.

CHAPTER 19
Dressing for Dinner

The western light threw strong shadows across the restaurant in the Portemilio. Per Prince Adbul El Fashid's orders, orchids bent over the table, a large table in a booth with dark red curtains in the candlelit room. The staff had created origami flowers, too, from white cotton napkins and had placed the silver settings over a mauve tablecloth. Set in the Kaslik coastal district near the tourist sites, the old hotel had been a resort stop for celebrities, so the wait staff there was accustomed to requests like the prince's, and from his demands, the waiters understood that the diners there tonight were special guests. This meant, of course, special tips. And in turn, this simultaneously meant any upsetting event would create a cacophony in discussions that would tarnish the hotel's pristine reputation. In other words, should the guests not be pleased, the place would likely encounter problems with the city's licensing department. So the *maitre d'* had selected the most obsequious waiters in the place to attend to the prince, Chelsey and Michael. By the time they'd arrived at the hotel and Ishmael had ushered them to their rooms, the dressmaker waited in the hall lobby to complete Chelsey's ensemble. At first, this resulted in confusion. "I didn't order a tailor,"

Chelsey had protested. "And I brought a dinner dress along with my suits. Perhaps room service can iron it. Or at least, bring me an iron."

"*Non!*" the woman replied. Obviously, she wouldn't been easily swayed. For one thing, she was French, with the stereotypical temperament and obstinacy of a French businesswoman, and she refused to give up what likely would be her highest-paying order this week. "*Le Prince—le prince, il demande cette!*" the middle-aged woman repeated again and again, until even strong-willed Chelsey gave into her. At first, she wondered why the prince had ordered a seamstress for her. Perhaps because she was meeting Michael when Ishmael kidnapped them, the prince had assumed she was a model. Had he seen her, he would've known she wasn't. She stood only five-foot-four and her head was too big to be a fashion model. Besides, if this was the prince's standard M.O., Chelsey gleaned this woman might have fashioned garments for Isadora. *This could be an opportunity*, she considered. Afterwards, she was thankful she'd surrendered, especially when she realized she likely would've been under-dressed for the occasion. She wasn't used to wearing long skirts or dresses, and although the sand-colored silk shift with the matching blazer would have been *appropo* for most sophisticated New York eateries—and certainly overdressed for most restaurants in her home city, it would have failed to meet the unspoken dress code for the hotel's dining room. Already, the dressmaker had constructed most of the dress and needed only to fit it to Chelsey. And even though the young investigator had often scoffed at such lavish displays of opulence, she admitted she enjoyed being privately fitted for a personally designed gown as if she were a duchess. So once she'd agreed to allow the woman create her evening's attire, the two of them worked together with Chelsey holding the tape measure, while the dressmaker, pins between her teeth, tucked and gathered, as if she had worked for Chelsey all of her life. She wanted the dressmaker to feel that way. It was crucial that the woman confide in her: Chelsey had to glean crucial information.

After twenty minutes or so, Chelsey made her move. Using an awkward combination of French and English, she asked the dressmaker if she'd put together gowns for all of the prince's women friends. She tried to keep her tone as nonchalant as possible.

The woman looked up at Chelsey's face, as if to judge from her expression just how close she was to the prince. "*Je ne sais pas.*" The woman pulled out pins from her lips. "*Mais c'est possible.*"

Chelsey explained that another friend of hers, Isadora, was also the prince's friend. "*Oui,*" she replied, she'd created a number of gowns for *la Deesse*, who was as charming *comme elle est belle*, within the past four months. But the woman was vague about Isadora's whereabouts. If the French women wasn't lying, apparently, sometimes the Goddess stayed at the prince's quarters in Beirut. Other times, she took up living in another palace, perhaps in Saudi Arabia. About this, the dressmaker admitted she was unsure. And the woman claimed she outfitted Isadora only during her Beirut stays. Mentally, Chelsey chewed upon the woman's words, "the last four months." So Isadora had spent time with the prince quite a while before her "disappearance."

These Scrabble pieces were not adding up—the words they formed didn't make sense. *Was Isadora's alleged disappearance a publicity stunt? Had Michael helped orchestrate this purported abduction to attract readers to his rag? If so, how cheap of him to drag Jack into the scheme. Or had Jack willingly joined Michael in the subterfuge?* She considered the last idea for a few minutes. Finally, she worried that all the surreal stress the past two days had driven her into paranoia. After all, even if Michael were involved in such an artifice, surely Jack wouldn't lower himself to it.

With her rusty French, Chelsey continued chatting with the woman until she had finished the fitting. Then, while the dressmaker tacked and sewed the alterations, Chelsey bathed and stretched her legs out full-length in the sunken marble tub. After she heard the old woman complete the gown, hang it, and leave, squeezing the door shut behind her, Chelsey stumbled upon a frightening realization: The dressmaker was the French-speaking woman in her dream. So Chelsey wondered just what bus she was riding now. *And where was this vehicle taking her?* She closed her eyes and tried to clean out her mind with the smell of the gardenia bubble bath and the warm bubbles that rose around her body and floated across her breasts. She squeezed a wash cloth and dripped the suds on her chest and stomach, then on her legs.

Decked out in a tux, Michael appeared years younger than he had that afternoon. Chelsey noted that he seemed more rested, or at least, calmer, as if he'd submitted to the situation. But she also noticed that he'd tried to comb over his receding hairline, and one thin, wayward tuft of hair poked out, giving him the appearance of a cockatoo. She drew a hand to her mouth to hide her giggle.

"What?" he asked. "You think I look like a penguin?"

She shook her head and tried to pat down the obstinate hair.

"Oh, my cowlick."

Right, Chelsey thought but said nothing and took his left arm just before they entered the dining room. Already, Prince Abdul El Fashid waited at their table. Chelsey had seen small black and white photos of him here and there, so she recognized him. But she had to admit, the newspaper prints hadn't done the man justice. His rugged skin made him appear more masculine, and his dark, intense eyes exuded a charisma that hadn't showed up in the photos. His white suit made his tan more pronounced, and as he smoked and flicked an ash, he moved with a grace she hadn't often seen in a man. Of course, she hadn't spent much time around royalty. At least, not in such close vicinity. As they approached the table, she wondered if etiquette demanded she curtsy. But then, considering that she'd been coerced into the meeting, she then decided, no, she wouldn't, unless Michael bowed. He didn't but nodded slightly before pulling out her chair. Immediately, one of the waiters took the chair from him and slid it under Chelsey while another pulled out Michael's.

"Welcome, my friends, to Beirut." His voice, low and throaty, seemed sincere enough, but Chelsey didn't like him referring to them as "his friends." She smiled slightly as she took her seat but declined to say anything. He appeared to be taken aback with her lack of verbal response. He raised himself higher in his seat, stiffened his torso, and inhaled deeply.

"Good evening," Michael said. "I pray Your Grace is doing well?"

Oh brother, Chelsey thought. He's laying it on thick. She focused upon the carvings in a silver butter knife. The geometric designs reminded her of those on a ring she once owned that was purportedly decorated with a miniature Aztec calendar. She ran a forefinger over its edges. Then she remembered that Islam allowed only geometric designs in all artwork. Nothing was to depict a representation of beings in this world—or in the world above.

"Quite well." Prince Abdul El Fashid nodded at Michael then focused upon Chelsey, who finally raised her eyelids and looked at him. "Does Ms. McKay like the gown?"

Chelsey smiled. "It's fine. Beautiful." *Actually, within her limited time frame, the dressmaker had performed extremely well. The woman had worked terribly hard,* Chelsey thought but said no more. She could not be that easily bought. Besides, the stitches underneath Chelsey's arms rubbed her flesh so she didn't feel quite comfortable. She hoped the stitches wouldn't break her skin.

"And Madame Loiselle? She was attentive and courteous?" He smiled, then took a drag from his cigarette.

Yes." Chelsey nodded. "Very professional." She glanced at the water goblet then back at him. She wanted to make a point without insulting him. "But I really wasn't expecting her."

The prince frowned slightly. "I have often heard that American women like sweet surprises." He tugged on an ear. "Is this not true?"

She tilted up her chin. "I'd say yes, generally, that's right." She wondered when—or if—this man would speak to her in a normal tone instead of this incessant lilting voice that sounded so patronizing. *Did he think she was an imbecile just because she'd allowed herself to become snared into this situation? Or perhaps he spoke to all women that way.* She pursed her lips, then continued. "It's very odd to be abducted, then imprisoned in a hotel room, then later, to be outfitted for a sophisticated dinner. All within thirty-six hours. It's strange, don't you think?"

The prince frowned. "Has anyone harmed you? Has Ishmael—"

"No." Now Chelsey lifted her torso and arched her back slightly. "Not physically. Again, I don't like being drugged and shoved onto a plane, headed to a country I'd never planned to see, then being caged in a room—no matter how polite the assailant may be." She picked up a water glass, sipped from it, then set it down firmly. "Now, you ask me how I'm doing, as if I'd received some social invitation and had elected to come to this place. I mean, *get real.*"

"Get *real?*" The prince widened his eyes. He could not speak for a few seconds, almost a minute. Finally, he said, "I see. " He closed his eyes and nodded. "And I apologize. Did Ishmael not tell you that I consider both of you guests? With all of my heart, I did not mean to cause you any stressfulness. I did not mean for you to suffer in any manner. It is just that there is such a need for confidentiality—"

"Confidentiality?" Michael asked. "For what?"

"Why?" Chelsey asked.

The prince's expression remained solemn. In fact, the corners of his lips sagged and his eyes grew wider. Chelsey noted that his pupils looked so much deeper that it appeared he had empathy for Michael and her. He frowned slightly before he spoke again. "My friends, you have been chosen—not by me, but by my contractors, for a wonderful excursion. One that will benefit *all* humankind. Again, I apologize for using such unsavory, even brutish methods to bring you here. This is a—how would you say it?—a *covert* operation. And yet, it is in the best interest of not only both of our countries, but in the best interest of our whole world."

"Contractors?" Michael asked. "Who are they? Not builders, I'm sure. Are they terrorists?"

"Oh, no." The prince knit his eyebrows. "Not at all. Quite the opposite, in fact. But at present, I am not at liberty to name them."

"Arabs?"

The prince shook his head. "No—I can tell you that much. But please do not question me further. Again, I cannot yet tell you these things." Then he swooped his right hand across the table. "Please—let all this show you that I am trustworthy. I took you from your homeland, yes. But I mean you no harm. I will see that every person on my staff will meet your every need."

"Except our freedom," Chelsey quipped.

For that, the prince had no answer, and for a few minutes, he said nothing, but sat there, looking glum. Finally, he turned toward Michael and asked, "Would you feel more comfortable about the situation if you stayed in my local palace? Would you trust me then—and see yourselves as my guests?"

Michael glanced at Chelsey, who returned his puzzled expression, then he looked back at the prince. "We need to think about that." he said. "And Ms. McKay and I must discuss it—in private—first."

The prince smiled slowly, nodded toward one of the waiters, who, with an agitated stance akin to a racehorse waiting for a gate to open, perched on a stool nearby. Abdul smiled and continued, "Come then, let us eat, drink, and be merry." He looked at Chelsey. "My dark butterfly—I would want no harm to come to your lithe and tawny limbs."

Dark butterfly? Lithe and tawny limbs? Chelsey glared at him a minute, then she focused upon her water glass and ran a finger around its rim. It made but a faint sound. *Was this guy for real? He asked them to trust him and then he put the make on her. On the other hand, perhaps merely he'd been reading too much poetry,* she wondered. But she said nothing.

Surprisingly, the dinner consisted of more than Mideastern food. Even though neither Michael nor Chelsey ordered them, trays holding a standing rib roast ringed with sautéed carrots and huge mounds of mashed potatoes. Apparently, the prince had thought the standard American dishes would appease and impress his guests. When the waiters unloaded the trays, Chelsey turned to Michael and said, "Oh. I'd *so* looked forward to a rack of lamb and couscous."

Michael drew up a hand to sh-sh her, but she rattled on. "And falafel. I'd so wanted to eat it again."

The prince stared at her and squinted. Then he waved a hand over the food. "You heard her. Take this away. Bring what she wants."

Chelsey raised her eyebrows and stared at Michael. Then she grinned. Perhaps this Prince Abdul wasn't totally a chauvinist. Or if he were, he attempted to be charming about it. Nevertheless, she would deem him to be a megalomaniac, except the man had no delusions of wealth, power or grandeur. He was wealthy, powerful and lived in grandeur. So it still irritated her even more that this prince, who never suffered a worldly need in his life, had the audacity to view other humans as merely beings he could twist and bend to his will, whether or not he had jurisdiction over them.

On the other hand, he was an Arab man. Once, long ago, she'd read a book, *The Arab Mind.* There, the author explained how young, wealthy Arab men, especially in Saudi Arabia, were raised to believe the world rotated around them. Indeed, the first few years of their lives, it did. They had wet nurses until after their third year, and maids fondled their genitalia and treated them as if they were the center of the universe. In contrast, female babies were weaned within the first year and learned to compete for attention—and then, they received far less than their brothers. Knowing this helped Chelsey make sense of the Mideast crisis that had lasted since she could remember. *Saddam Hussein, Osama bin Laden, Ayatola Komeni—all of them were spoiled Arab boys who'd never learned to share. And this prince merely grabbed people away from their lives to join him in his palace and for what?* Other than what she read in the book, she knew little about this world. So she wondered if the prince's actions were normal for the culture. Perhaps here, kidnapping was the standard M.O. for royalty.

When she was an adolescent in the early nineties, Neil had forbidden her to go to shopping malls alone. "Make sure you're never in a john alone, either," he said, his eyes growing large. "Girls have been kidnapped and sold in slave markets in the Mideast." He'd claimed the week before, cops had caught kidnappers who'd knocked out a fourteen-year-old, shaved her hair, and stuffed her in a plastic bag, while her girlfriend waited for her outside the restroom. At the time, Chelsey and her friends, behind Neil's back, of course, laughed about his threatening story. They were sure he repeated some cheesy urban legend. Today, Chelsey wasn't so sure. *Perhaps the stories were true. Perhaps that is what happened to Isadora, but she was thwarted from revealing that to Michael. Perhaps that is what was happening to Michael and her, too.*

She watched the waiters carry away the steaming trays, smells of the beef and potatoes wafting behind. Probably, she would've loved the meal. But no way, would she allow the prince to so easily assuage his guilt. No, he would suffer. That is, if he had any guilt or harbored *any* true compassion for his species. *No!* Winning her trust would not be easy, if it were even possible. After all, the man had ordered her to be kidnapped—and now, he wouldn't even discuss why. *The male Arab mind. Exotic, yes, but oh, so strange. And oh, so chauvinistic.*

Suddenly, a tall, black-haired woman stepped out of a booth kitty-cornered from them. She wore a tight black, lacy blouse, a flowing skirt, and stiletto sling-backs. She stared at the booth where waiters scurried away with trays piled high, waddled back to it, her heels clacking on the tile floors, and drew back the curtains. She stared at the prince and frowned. "You are here?" She withdrew a hand from the curtain and crossed her arms. "And hardly alone."

The prince wrinkled his forehead. "There must be some mistake."

"This is no mistake—I was to meet you here." Now, Fatima stood, arms akimbo, pressing her knuckles into her hips and started clacking one of her heels.

Chelsey drew a napkin over her mouth to hide her smile. In fact, she clenched a corner of it in between her teeth to keep from laughing. *So the playboy was caught in one of his seductive schemes*, she thought. But she said nothing, only continued struggling to suppress her laughter. Certainly, this woman must be one of his girlfriends to be so bold as to confront him at his table. She looked at Michael, who seemed amused. The corners of his mouth curled upward. But quickly, he grabbed his wine and sipped it.

The prince's tawny face turned livid. "I am so sorry, Madam. But indeed, this is a mistake, some miscommunication.

Meanwhile, *the maitre d'* saw the disruption and stared for a minute, his face glazed with horror. Immediately, he scurried to the table. "Oh, Your Highness, I am so sorry. I should have sent this woman away."

"Sent away, indeed!" Fatima stomped her foot. Her face grew nearly as red as the floral design in her skit. "Ishmael el-Haddid sent me here—and he owes me money for it. Now, I am shamed! For doing my job."

When Chelsey heard Ishmael's name, she felt compassion for the woman and her situation. She dropped her napkin. "Please have her join us," she said, first looking at the prince, then the *maitre d'*. "We have plenty of room here. And obviously, she was merely following orders. She should not be punished. Already, she's been embarrassed. That's unfair." Then Chelsey looked at the woman. "That is, if you would still want to join us."

Speechless upon hearing such reasoning and such kind words of understanding, Fatima stared at Chelsey a long time. She lowered her arms and her chest sunk. She looked at the appetizers on the table. Although she'd nibbled at those the waiter had brought her—some humus and pita bread, that was nothing like what these people were eating—cheeses, spinach and artichoke dips and even shrimp tails. Her mouth nearly watered. Finally, ignoring the men and staring at Chelsey, she replied in a soft voice. "Thank you so much for your kindness. But you are a lady. I am a poor working woman. No, I should not embarrass you by sitting at your table. It would not be right. It would be rude."

Chelsey frowned. "You will not embarrass us. Don't be silly. Come, sit down."

Fatima smiled, tears rimmed her eyes, and she shook her head. "No. I appreciate very much your offer. But I know my station." Then, she stiffened a minute. "But that Ishmael—he will pay me double!" With that, she whirled around, stopped at her booth to pick up her purse, and proudly stomped out of the restaurant.

His eyes gleaming even more intensely, the prince looked at Chelsey and smiled. "You are most kind, so considerate of this woman who is such an underling."

Chelsey glared at him. "It seems to me that many men, especially in *your* country, see *all* women as underlings. Call it my act toward sisterhood."

He reached for one of her hands. "Please, I mean to compliment you. Yes, our customs are different. But please do not be offended by my words."

She smiled a little when he touched her hand. Then, she sighed and looked at Michael. She must take Michael aside and talk with him.

Michael shrugged and shook his head. Then, he picked up his wine. "To all of us," he said. "In this crazy world. May we figure it out soon."

Later, after the prince had escorted Chelsey to a room and finally left her alone, she slipped out and scurried down the hall to Michael's suite. When she rapped on the door, Michael opened it quickly, and she entered his room.

"I think I've figured it out."

Michael knit his eyebrows.

"Why we were kidnapped." She inhaled deeply. "I bet the prince is a part of a cult. Remember the Hale Bopp comet in 1997? Heaven's Gate?"

"You may be right." Michael sighed. "But I hope not. That didn't go well."

CHAPTER 20
Rendez-vous

José Garcia sat at a narrow bar and watched the plump derriere of a waitress in a long, dark skirt. The skirt wrinkled at her hips when she bent over to bus a table. He leaned to one side of the stool, hoping to catch a shot of her breasts when she bent the other way. He looked back at the counter when the bartender poured him a shot of Hiram's 7 and positioned the bottle beside it. José nodded, but remembered he had to keep his mind focused, if not on his job, on this meeting. He glanced at his watch. One-fifteen p.m. His old American buddy should be showing up any minute. He sighed. He hadn't seen Jack in at least ten years, although the two of them phoned each other every few months. Sometimes, he'd give Jack a lead on a story. Other times, Jack came across a piece of info or story that helped one of José's investigations. Today, he wondered what Jack might have heard about the fast food bombings here—and if he had any leads. Even though José's team had been tailing the rebels for eight months now, the bombings had caught them off-guard. Of course, he couldn't let Jack know that. Instead, he'd have to probe the newspaper man for information. Funny, he thought, how sometimes news went to other countries before it circulated here.

Most of the Beirut citizens hadn't heard of the bombings yet, unless they'd been in the vicinity or knew someone who saw them. Or saw someone wounded by one of the bombs. It happened far too often around here, probably as much as in Iraq or Afghanistan.

He didn't like this city much, but it was one of the hottest places for getting promoted. After another year, at the most, two, he'd return to the states, maybe take it easy in the D.C. office till he retired. Then, at least, it'd be with a bigger pension. But he had to make good here— and so far, he wasn't happy with his record. Two bombings. Thirty-five civilians wounded, two of them dead. No, it didn't look good. And he was getting too old for this—chasing terrorists, meeting cronies in cheap dives, watching his back with every move. Certainly, he belonged back in a cushy office in some high rise like Ballston Towers in Arlington—or maybe the Stouffer's Building in Crystal City. He tossed down a shot, and heard the door screech open. He looked at it.

Finally, Jack sauntered into the bar. The newspaperman slapped José on the back. "What's up, my man?"

"Still at it." José motioned for the bartender to bring another glass, and he poured Jack a shot. "So how's the love-nest?"

"Dee-Dee's fine." Jack threw down the shot and sighed. "Except she's pissed about me coming here. Whew! Is she ever."

"Hey, man. You haven't been on the road in a while—"

"Ten years." Jack poured himself another shot and tipped the bottle toward José, who nodded. "And I wouldn't have come this time. But like I told you—this kid's my top reporter, and I got her into this." He put down the bottle and drew his pipe out of his sports coat pocket, then filled it with tobacco. "You find out anything?"

"Maybe." José slipped a cigarette out of his pack on the bar. "You said she's young? Red-head? Freckles?"

Jack puffed on his pipe. "More auburn. Freckles? I dunno. Not so you'd notice them—you know, like the real redheaded ones. I brought a pic." Jack dug in his lapel pocket and drew out a snapshot of Chelsey. "Pretty recent. Last few months. Our photographer took it for her press card."

"Cute kid." José stared at the photo and fingered it awhile, as if he were trying to pick up her essence. "Looks young."

"I dunno. Twenty-three, twenty-four." Jack sighed and shook his head. "First job out of J-school. Gutsy kid, too. I told her to take a cab to Michael's office. But she insisted he meet her at LaGuardia to save time—so they could get moving, get on a plane if they had to, to look for Isadora, the fashion model who disappeared."

"The Granite Goddess?"

Jack nodded.

"She's here."

Jack stared at him. "Why didn't you tell anyone back home? What's going on?" José chuckled and shook his head. "She hasn't been nabbed.

She's doing quite well. She came here by choice and she's staying in one of Prince Abdul El Fashid's penthouses here in the city."

"Why did the agency let everyone think she'd been kidnapped?"

José shrugged then leaned back on his stool. "The politics here are kinda strange. If some of this prince's customers find out he's harboring an American sweetie, they might cut off trade. Lotsa people here don't like you folks."

"That isn't news." Jack relit his pipe. "This have something to do with the bombings?"

"Could be, in a sense." José glanced at the waitress and then looked at Jack. "Terrorists did the bombings, we know that much. But that's not what I mean. I'm talking about businessmen. The way I figure it, the prince has to watch his image because of his trade with the Arab Coalition. And we aren't sure yet—there might be terrorists' tie-ins with them. It's very covert." José poured another shot and offered one to Jack, who took it. "Even if there's no terrorist connection, outside of Beirut and Saudi Arabia, a lot of Arab businessmen don't want to get too close to the U.S. And they cut back on trading—you know, giving the best prices and so on—with those who don't nuzzle up to the Americans. That's why people like the prince—or actually, his dad, have set up branches here. They play both sides—trade with the West from their palaces and offices in Saudi Arabia, and they trade with their buddies and family from palaces and offices in other Arab states.

They just have to be careful who knows what. So the prince might not want his anti-American contractors to know he's housing a beautiful American model."

"And he wants it to look like terrorists nabbed Isadora?" Jack put down his shot. "And he's got the money to keep you guys off him?"

"With the agency, it isn't money that talks." José inhaled a long drag. "But he's got something on someone, I'll bet, 'cause we were told everything was hush-hush. We don't say anything about the Goddess. So I figure it's all got to do with business."

"Makes sense. Follow the money," Jack mumbled and stared into the distance awhile, then looked back at José. "So has anyone seen Chelsey?"

"Soon as you called, I put a team on the Kaslik district. It's a tourist trap, but it's also close to the Portemilio. The prince owns stock in that hotel. And if he knew—or heard—Chelsey was after Isadora for an interview, he might have had her snatched."

"So what do we need to do to get her back?" Jack squinted. "Pay a ransom?"

"A ransom?" José laughed. "From one of the richest men in the world?" Then, he laughed harder and harder, so hard, tears flowed. "I was thinking we'd wire the place to find out if she's there."

Jack frowned then chewed on his pipe. "That's legal here? I mean, without probable cause for a warrant?"

José nodded. "Don't need it under the FISA." He blew a smoke ring. It hovered in the air awhile before it dispersed.

"Just say it was foreign surveillance, right?" Jack smirked.

José nodded. "Who knows? He may be planning something against the U.S. Especially if he's keeping our citizens hostage."

Jack pursed his lips. "Hostages? God, I hope not."

José shrugged. "I don't know what to tell you. This seems strange to me. Very strange. And in this miserable excuse for a city, I've seen about everything."

"Thought I had, too." Jack sighed deeply, then he slumped like a man defeated, pulled out his pipe, and set it on the counter. He glanced around the bar area and noticed the waitress still busing tables. "How's the food in this joint? Are they still serving? I'm starved."

CHAPTER 21
Up in the Air Again

Dardiel and Liwet finished measuring the walls of the laboratory and stopped to go over their calculations. Soon, several energetic Serkerpians would help them change out the synthetic steel siding with the mirrored glass. The ship would be ready within ten days, at the most, eleven, Dardiel estimated, because the glass fit perfectly. While other Serkerpians removed the walls, the two of them would position the glass. Everything, as Dardiel had anticipated, was flowing along on schedule. Now the two of them prepared to talk with Emeth about Michael Levine. And the idea frightened Liwet quite a bit.

"Perhaps he'll think we're questioning him, and then—I fear his wrath." Liwet shivered and his wings flickered wildly. In fact, they flickered so much, a few thin wisps of fluff floated in the air then drifted to the laboratory floor.

"Not if we approach the situation wisely." Dardiel had spoken with Emeth more often than Liwet. "I know him to be slow to anger. We will let him know we were just checking to ensure no mistakes will occur. Our primary duty is to be his messengers. He will respect us for doing that: following our mission, our orders. Besides, he will be able to discern why the two earthlings share such a similar DNA." He smiled. "And quite frankly, I would like to know the answer to that mystery."

Liwet settled down a bit. "You're right, I suppose. You are so much wiser about political and philosophical issues. My specialty's romance and invention." He sighed. "Which reminds me, have you noticed a change in Miss McKay?"

Dardiel nodded and smiled. "Yes. It appears the citadel around her mosaic heart has begun to weaken. Even if I cannot see it, as Emeth can, I noticed a lightness in her step when we viewed her yesterday. And her eyes glimmer more brightly. She smiles wider now, too."

"I worry that she may be attracted to Michael." Liwet frowned. "Not only is he too old for her, but there *is* the DNA concern." Then, he paused and stared into the distance. "But perhaps, she's attracted to the prince. Then we needn't worry about the DNA. On the other hand, the prince has been such a cad with women."

"True." Dardiel glowed more brightly. "But he has been changing. Lately, many events have humiliated him. Many mishaps have been purifying him, enabling him to truly love, to go beyond imitating that act. No true lover lacks compassion."

"Hey—that's my territory.

"Sorry." Dardiel smiled. "I did not mean to invade it. Nevertheless, truth is Truth, regardless of whether one's specialty is with romance or philosophy. And so often, they overlap." Dardiel winked at Liwet then picked up a corner of one of the mirrored-glass segments. "Here, help me carry this to the ceiling."

Liwet picked up the other end, and the two set it in place. Afterwards, they did the same with each segment, positioning the pieces where they would eventually be attached. They stood back and looked at the mirror segments one more time.

"That will do until the others remove the siding," Dardiel said and clicked his wings. "Now, to Emeth."

The two of them swooped out of the laboratory, glided higher, and then soared higher into the heavens. They darted around each other awhile, playing their game of skip-and-pass, until finally, they flew parallel to each other like jets at an air show. The further they flew, the stronger they glowed with the sun's rays highlighting their forms. Had some *homo sapiens* seen them, they likely would have declared the two Serkerpians to be comets streaking across a noon-day sky. But they flew too far from earthling eyes—even those viewing the heavens with telescopes containing the highest magnifying lenses. Finally, they arrived at the mansion above a hilltop of clouds, where the colors of the sky were so fluorescent, so intense, viewing them would sting earthling eyes. They landed just outside the gate, where the guard Wisdom sat reading *The Dictionary of American Slang*. Her fair, blonde hair draped her shoulders like a *hijab* while she pored over the book. Every so often, she would lift her face from the pages and stare into space. But when she saw Liwet and Dardiel, she drew fingers through her hair as if to beckon them and smiled. They nodded and waved but didn't stop.

"She's such so lovely," Liwet said. "Like a dream. Why can't we spend time talking with her? Certainly, it would not do us any harm."

"No, we must hurry." Dardiel laughed. "I thought you were the impatient one."

"Only sometimes. She inspires me so. We should talk with her more often."

"Next time—we shall plan on it."

They hovered over the walkway leading into the structure, then entered the huge foyer, where they stopped to check-in with Emeth's secretary, Melchisedek. The secretary was a being taller than even Dardiel, who was quite a tall Serkerpian.

"Go on in." Melchisedek smiled. "He is expecting you."

Folding their wings behind them, they entered the throne room. They bowed to Emeth when they entered the throne room. He did not acknowledge them at first. Sitting on a sardonyx and jasper throne, Emeth played chess with himself. He looked up a few seconds after they stepped under the doorjamb arching twelve feet above them.

"Welcome, my friends." He smiled, and the room grew white with shimmery light, whiter than an earthling has ever seen, a blinding white, a halogen white, a laser white, a white so strong it enveloped the entire room, a white that to even Dardiel and Liwet seemed like the inside of a giant snowball, except with it, came a warmth that would melt the polar ice caps in one swoop. "How can I help you today?"

Dardiel spoke first. "Your Highest, we have come to discuss what may possibly be a discrepancy in the list for the colony ship we have been assembling."

"A discrepancy?" Emeth set down a pawn and drew a hand to his chin. "Of course, you are always welcome here. But I find it unusual you did not e-mail me about this discrepancy."

"Yes, Your Grace, that would have been more efficient. However, I have brought the entire list—at least, the one up to today's earthly date—and I thought we might re-check each name, just to ensure everything is in order."

Emeth smiled again. "Essentially, you are most concerned about Mr. Michael Levine, are you not?"

Embarrassed they had been so vain to not anticipate that Emeth would immediately know their concerns, long before they had spoken them, Dardiel and Liwet reddened as they nodded.

"His DNA is too close to Ms. McKay's, correct? And along with the elderly and children, we planned to take those who might choose to procreate. But we must ensure only viable unions will occur, correct? So you are worried something will go awry?" Then Emeth laughed, shaking the entire mansion, rocking the chandeliers back and forth as if they were pendulums, sending the paintings out-of-kilter, rattling even the windows. And the light that streamed forth from him shone even whiter than before. "You need not fret. He is Chelsey's father. She will learn this before the trip."

"Thank you, Your Highness, Your Grace," the two chimed in unison.

"I remain Emeth to you." The King smiled again. Once again, the room flowed with white light. "I am not angry—merely faintly amused. Do not fret, little ones. Everything is moving along as I had planned." He looked back at his chess board, then used a white pawn to jump a black queen. "Ah, ha! Check. And a certain check-mate. Sartarel loses this round." Emeth raised his head and glanced around. "He's hiding again today. He must come out to receive his fate."

Dardiel and Liwet also glanced around, but didn't see the fallen angel. They were especially glad they did not today. Both of them felt backslidden. So with cheeks still flushed, Dardiel and Liwet took their humble leave. They nodded, bowed low, and backed out of the throne room, nearly stumbling over their long gowns. Once back in the foyer, Liwet nudged Dardiel and whispered, "I told you we should have taken time to talk with her. It always pays."

So the two stopped at the gate.

Wisdom lifted her face. "You appear saddened. But you have merely been humbled. Since when is humility such a negative event or experience? It must carry some merit because it helps an entity learn."

Then she smiled broadly and winked. "And I have noticed that it nearly always brings you to me."

Liwet sighed. "I have been so faithless, so disrespectful." Suddenly, he melted into a lump at her feet. "As if I have been a rebel."

She stared at him a few seconds. "Did Emeth say that?"

"Well, no. He said he was faintly amused."

She smiled and patted the top of Liwet's head. "Then, that is the Truth. Emeth *never* lies." She hugged each of them, then rubbed the back of Liwet's neck. "You have done well, you two. But you must review the guide book. Remember, he is faithful when we are not. And if he forgives us, we must forgive ourselves."

"Yes, yes, of course." Liwet brightened and began radiating light again. So did Dardiel, who'd remained silent while Wisdom spoke. After they chatted for a while longer, the two soared off, again darting around each other, diving and whirling. They flew in wild geometric patterns, crisscrossing each other's flight lines, they created almost imperceptible figure eights—or the signs of infinity—across the skies, all the way back to the laboratory ship. There, they landed softly, entered the ship and went back to work.

CHAPTER 22
Elevated on Earth

Heavy laden with feelings of humiliation, the prince dragged his feet and hung his head slightly when he trudged back to his room. He took the stairs to avoid anyone he might meet on the elevator. With the late dinner, he had decided to spend the night in a Portemilio suite. Tomorrow morning, he would take a taxi to the office. But tonight, he had wanted to avoid his butler and servants, spend his evening alone or with the charming American. Had the dinner gone better, Miss McKay likely would be joining him here for a nightcap and perhaps an hour of whispers and glances. So he had sent his manservant back to the palace. Now, he went by himself to an empty, lonely room. Usually, staying at the hotel lifted his spirits, but it tonight, it did not. The hallways seemed dark, gloomy, almost like catacombs or perhaps a dungeon. He smelled mildew, and he halfway expected to stumble across bones, grayed and brackish from years of lying in a dank, underground cave.

He wondered if he should give up reading, reciting, and writing poetry—perhaps it had wrought him such disrespect. No more did the world hold poetry sacred, did it see this talent as a sign of virility, a sign from Allah that such a person with this talent was one of Allah's special messengers. Today, the prince contended, the world merely laughs at poets, leaves them stranded in streets, lying face-down in mud, as damaged and worthless as the wrist corsage he had purchased for Miss McKay. With these dark feelings and having walked down such a dimly-lit hallway, he was astonished after he slipped in his key and stepped into his suite.

It was light, so light, and such a white-blue light—all colors together—that hit him so hard, the prince squinted and drew up a hand to shade his eyes. He became even more puzzled when he noticed the lamps threw down no light on the end tables. Obviously, the lamps had not been lit. He glanced at the ceiling. The tiny bulbs in the chandelier were not lit, either, and so he looked around for the source of the light. Like white flames, it filtered out from the bedroom, outlining the closed door. Had something caught fire there, he wondered. *Such a capstone that would be to such an already horrible day*, he thought. Keeping a hand above his eyes, he hesitantly moved toward the door, then fearful of what he would find, he flung it open and hopped back, as if to dodge a bullet. There, in the bedroom, stood one of the beings he had encountered in his jet six months before. Bent over the prince's mud-soaked suit that he had folded over a chair, the being rubbed a hand over the garment, and *voila!* The mud dried up and disintegrated into dust, and the prince's clothes were suddenly clean, even pressed, as if they'd just arrived from a dry cleaners, without, of course, the plastic bag.

Prince Abdul El Fashid did not know quite what to say. After muttering, "Thanks," he stood there a minute, squinting. Then awed, he fell to his knees.

The being whirled around and smiled. "Hello, again, Abdul."

Squinting harder from the beam of light the being shot from his smile, the prince stammered, "Hello," and continued shading his eyes with a hand. Gradually, he mustered up the courage to ask, "Why have you come? I am gathering those persons together as you asked. Have I done something wrong?"

The being laughed a loud, ringing, echoing laugh that shook the room. "No more than usual. And actually, perhaps less than you have in days past." He moved closer to the prince and fluttered his wings. "Do get up. You are not to worship me."

The prince blinked. "Oh, uh, sorry. I am just so astounded. Today has not been a day I want to remember."

"Oh no?" The being flapped his wings and crossed its arms. "You are wrong my friend. This will be a day you will revere for eternity. You have progressed further than even I had anticipated within so few hours."

"I have?" The prince shook his head. "No, not today. All day, I have merely played the buffoon."

"Yes!" The being clapped its hands. "And what is more—you have come to realize it." The being pressed a palm on one of Prince El

Fashid's shoulders and squeezed it slightly. "That is the greatest difference. You see, my friend, you have no more played the fool today than on any other day. In fact, less so, because you have arrived at this epiphany. When you fell in the street, soaked yourself in mud, you were far wiser than when you spent hours seducing women, pretending you cared for them, whispering nothings—which were truly nothings—to them, or when you transacted business deals to your advantage without thinking of your contractors' profits or welfare. Wiser than when you snapped at your man servants or maids, not because of anything they did, but because your mood was gray."

The prince had started to rise from his knees, but upon hearing these words, he sat back down and crossed his legs. Still squinting, although his eyes were growing accustomed to the light now, he stared at the being for a few minutes, then he shook his head. "I had no idea. I—"

"I know. You were so self-obsessed, you had no idea how others saw you. That is why I held so much hope for you. You did not mean to be a cruel tyrant. You simply were not aware of how others saw you, how you treated them."

The prince drew his fingers to his forehead. "Yes, I have truly been a fool."

The being shrugged. "No more than most *homo sapiens*. In fact, you have acted less the role than many of them have."

Slumped over, the prince stared at his feet and noticed a scuff on one of his loafers, then a thought occurred to him. It was a thought that offered him relief. He looked back at the being. "Such as my father?"

"Yes, your earthly, biological father."

The prince pursed his lips. "It is interesting. Now that you have said that, I no longer resent or hate him. I pity him. He, too, does not know what he is doing."

"*Tres bien!*" The being clicked his wings. "You have ventured one more step up the ladder."

"The ladder?"

"To the spiritual realm."

"Me?" The prince inhaled deeply and straightened his back. "I thought I must pray, meditate, or write poetry to climb such a ladder. And even though I have done these things, I have not done them diligently." He looked at the floor and sighed. "Most use these tools more wisely—and shelter themselves, which I have not done."

"Of course, all those tools help." The being shrugged and flickered his wings again. "But too many earthlings become lost in the methods and forget the goals, which these tools are meant to help them achieve. And when they shelter themselves from others, they become isolated— not necessarily a spiritual achievement."

"Hmmm." The prince scratched an ear and looked pensive. "I had not thought of it quite that way."

"You are still young." The being smiled. "Terribly young, and compared to an eternity, you are but a baby in the universe. So do not worry that you have not amassed centuries of wisdom."

"Somehow, I feel very old." The prince sighed. "And so alienated, so alone."

"Ah yes—Miss McKay." The being closed his wings, bent over, and placed his fingers under Prince Abdul's chin. "Do not worry about her, my friend. You have found more favor with her than you realize. In fact, more than what she yet realizes."

The prince gulped. "I have?" The prince eyes grew more intense. "I am surprised you concern yourself with what must be such a frivolous matter, that is, to your kind."

The being withdrew his hand and drew his thin eyebrows together. "Oh no. That is where you are wrong." He perched his hands on his hips. "And perhaps, although you fantasize about romance continually, you see it as frivolous, as superficial because you have had no concept of what true love entails. Man was not meant to live alone. We take the relationship between a man and woman most seriously. Our guide book details it within many sections."

The prince remained silent a few seconds, then he asked, "Is that why you came here tonight? To tell me these things?"

"Yes. But that is not my main message." The being smiled, and the glowing aura emanating from him spread larger. He became so bright that the prince once again cupped a hand over his eyes. "It is about the gathering. Although I have asked you to bring Isadora, Miss McKay, and Mr. Levine here, one more step remains, another step that is crucial."

"What is that?" The prince lowered his hand and knit his brows. His forehead wrinkled into an exaggerated quizzical expression, much like a basset hound's.

"You must bring them to Jerusalem, the meeting place." The being crossed his arms. "We will meet you there a week from the day after tomorrow."

"Jerusalem? The Holy City?"

"Of course. It is holy to all of us and to most earthly religions. Have you ever considered why?"

The prince shrugged.

The being shook his head. "Time enough later for that lesson. It is crucial that you be there—on Golgotha ten days from now—at seven forty-five p.m."

"Golgotha—the place of the skull?"

"Precisely."

The prince nodded. "I have one more question."

"Of course. We will give you the riyals when you have brought them to us."

"Good!" the being said. "We will have the money. I must go."

The prince blinked. "Actually, I had forgotten about that."

"What about my question?"

"Ah yes." The being smiled. "You may call me Gabriel. That is my name." With that, he clicked his wings again, flew to the window, which magically opened by itself, and the being soared into the evening sky. The prince stood at window, and his stare followed the being until it disappeared.

Then the prince stared out at the night sky. Suddenly, the stars seemed to dance, a lovely dance, so lovely that the prince was inspired to write a poem about them. He rushed to his bed where he kept pen and paper on an end table.

"The night is alive with dance," he scribbled.

The stars pirouette
and slip into a waltz.
Moving like candles
lit for a feast,
they slip across the sky
and form a staircase
of triangles
that lead to Heaven,
where they wait, steady.
They glimmer and wait
as tirelessly as
I wait for one smile
from your lips,
one look in your eyes.
They wait as I wait
for your love.

CHAPTER 23
Another Ring in the Circus

Ishmael turned the corner a bit too fast, and the rear end of the limo fish-tailed and swerved too far to the right. He glanced at the rear view mirror and spotted a car tailing him. It was a light green, Dodge Caravan. He was certain he'd seen the car the night before parked in bushes outside the stone entranceway to the prince's Beirut palace. Today, two men sat in the front seat. The driver was dark but the other had white hair and looked as if he could be an American. But with the morning light glaring in under the visors, it was hard to tell from this distance. Then again, perhaps this was a coincidence. Maybe, the men weren't following him. He would see, he decided and suddenly, turned left at the next street. He whizzed down it and kept glancing at the mirror. Soon, the van rumbled after him. Again, he worried. The kidnapping hadn't ceased to bother him, and perhaps, some authorities caught wind of it. The van looked innocuous, not likely to house G-men or policemen, but too many times, things weren't what they seemed. No telling who might be riding in the touristy looking vehicle.

He worried that American FBI men, working incognito, might be on his tail. Or even worse, the CIA. With the van closer now, he could see the men talking. The American-looking one smoked a pipe, and the other flicked cigarette ashes out of his cracked window. Okay, then, he thought, his best bet would be to lose them.

He passed one street, then at the next, turned right, then once he rounded the corner, a sharp left. He was moving toward the coastline now, where palm trees dappled the skyline, and many of the buildings looked the same. He'd lose them there, he hoped, and pushed harder on the accelerator. After zigzagging through more narrow streets, intermittently glancing at his mirror, he could no longer see the van, so he wound his way through different streets, taking another path back to the palace.

***

Two hours before, Jack and José had given up the chase. They figured Ishmael might be merely running an errand. When José spotted the limo, he wanted to tail it because he was sure it belonged to the prince and possibly, it'd lead them to Michael and Chelsey. He'd called Jack at seven a.m. that morning. "Just found out, one of my men saw a redhead in the prince's limo yesterday," José had said. So despite his hangover and lack of sleep, Jack met him to go along for the ride. But he was taken aback by the van.

"That's your vehicle?" He wrinkled his nose. "We're going in that? I like the idea of going undercover but really—"

José shrugged. "Not the classiest model. But indiscrete."

"It isn't the model so much." Jack wiped his mouth with the back of a hand then took another bite of a doughnut. "It's just the color."

José shrugged. "Comes with the territory. You know the feds and their penchant for green."

"Yeah." Jack smirked and shook his head.

After they'd lost Ishmael, they decided to stake out the palace all morning and parked behind bushes not far from the front gate, where they could see any vehicle coming into or leaving the grounds. A while later, a woman with long, dark hair and a flowing skirt disembarked from a taxi about fifty yards from the gate. She wore heavy makeup, and she kept smoothing her hair while she wobbled in high heels over the cobblestone drive leading up to the gate. Sometimes, she tilted left, then right, her large purse swinging, as she struggled across the rough trail. Every now and then, she'd glance right then left, drawing her hand to her forehead to shade her eyes. The two men concurred either she was meeting someone, or, they thought, she was lost. She looked out-of-place in the luxurious setting. They agree to drive up and help her.

José rolled down the window. "You meeting someone?"

"Maybe." The woman squinted and drew her shawl around her.

"Why do you ask? I am doing nothing illegal."

José wondered if he looked that much like a cop, especially today, when he was decked out in his tourist costume—Hawaiian shirt, khaki shorts, long, white socks. "No, Ma'am. Didn't mean to insinuate that. We just thought you might need help."

"Oh?" She smiled, showing a scarlet line across her upper teeth, where she had inadvertently applied lipstick. "Would you know a person who lives around here?"

"Who?"

"A Mr. Ishmael el-Haddid."

The men smiled. "We know where he lives—or at least, where he spends most of his days. You might say it's his employment address. Were you to meet him here?"

"Not exactly." She looked down and seemed to study the tires on the van, then, she raised a hand again to shade her eyes from the sun. "You see, I had a contract with him. I performed a service for his boss, and he has never paid me. Now, he owes me money. And I've come to collect."

"He does?" José elbowed Jack then leaned back and grinned broadly. "He most certainly should pay you. I think we saw him driving toward the coast. He drives a limo, right? Beige?"

She nodded twice.

"It's kinda hot today." José smiled again. "You're welcome to wait in our van."

She glared at each man, then eyed the wheels, the windows, and bumpers. Then, she looked back at José and squinted. "I don't know who you are, not even your names. You are asking me to sit in this crazy van of yours when you may be killers or rapists or who knows what?"

José smiled. "I'm José, and this is Jack, an American, visiting here for what—the second time?" He looked back at Jack, who nodded.

She shifted her weight from her left to her right, then back again. Studying them a minute more, she said. "Okay. It is warm. Thank you." Then she walked around to Jack's side. "Oh yes. My name is Fatima. Welcome to Lebanon."

CHAPTER 24
At Last, Romance?

Sweet smells of cinnamon and the white morning light woke Chelsey before her alarm went off. At least, she had her radio alarm again. Acting appalled when he'd learned of Ishmael's tactics, the prince had insisted it be returned, along with her watch and cell phone. Now, she pulled herself up and sat cross-legged on the canopy bed. She felt better this morning than she had for months. For once, she'd awakened without thrashing through the night. Indeed, she'd enjoyed a good night's sleep, the first one in a long time. A night's sleep that hadn't been flooded with nightmares. Still, she worried that she and Michael might be calves being fed for the slaughter. Who were the "contractors" who ordered the prince to abduct them? She's never learned about such antics in any articles she'd read on Islam. If the prince were part of a cult, surely she would find other members within the palace grounds. Or perhaps some of his servants might participate in the cult rituals. She decided today she would observe everyone within the hotel, especially the prince's servants.

She blinked and stretched, then picked up her bible from an end table and scanned it for sections Erica had marked. She was uncertain about the feelings arising inside her and hoped to find some guidance. Soon, she came across a verse circled in red and highlighted in yellow. Erica had scribbled a red asterisk beside it, too. "Say not ye, There are yet four months, and then cometh harvest? Behold, I say unto you, Lift up your eyes, and look on the fields: for they are white already to harvest."

It was in *John*, Chapter 4, Verse 35. She remembered the fields waving past the car window the day before and decided, yes, she understood why the bible contained so much agrarian imagery. Yes, it was here, in this very corner of the world, where all those stories took place. Perhaps, too, the bible and being in the Mideast helped her make sense, not only of the kidnappings, but of the twisted path she had trod for almost all of her life. It seemed most days filled with unnecessary stress and bathos. Even with the racing around to avoid Ishmael, the pace of life here was different.

Reflecting upon that thought made her nearly glad she was here, albeit kidnapped, even if, for no other reason, for the adventure of seeing a portion of the planet she wouldn't have likely opted to see. And she rather liked the scenery. Also the trip provided a pleasant relief from rushing to interview people—too many self-centered jerks, then write their stories, and finally, rush even more to keep on top of the rest of her life. It had become difficult to endure such arduous tasks as trips to drug stores and supermarkets. Any more, these excursions were horrid.

It wasn't that she disliked the act of shopping for groceries, picking out cheeses, fresh tomatoes, and maybe cookies. In fact, once she'd enjoyed the duty. But now, even in her small city, driving, shopping, almost everything had grown too hectic. Trying to keep on top of reporting duties and freelancing as an investigator made her life too rushed. And too often, the checkout episodes at the supermarket made her feel so insignificant. For example, when she might be in a hurry, the customer ahead of her would dawdle, spend several minutes writing a check, blabbering with the cashier, or sending clerks back for another bag of flour or for box of margarine. Or while she stood waiting, the cashier would let anyone and everyone interrupt him—or to open his drawer for change, to stop the line to change drawers, or to ask questions about other products and UPC codes. And even though she almost always prepared her checks ahead of time—except for the amount, of course—to be efficient, the clerk and customers behind her would then rush her, hurry her by ringing up a new customer's purchases long before she'd put away her change or had slipped her pen into its pocket.

So pen clenched between her teeth, she'd waddle toward the exit while carrying a receipt and a five-spot between her fingers, and she'd try to steer a cart with her elbows as she simultaneously clutched a thin plastic bag of groceries, always too heavy for the sack that inevitably started ripping at its seams. Generally, she'd collide with some person staring into space or at an I-pad, end up blocking the exit, not to be irritable or to exhibit some Aphrodite complex, but merely because she required a few seconds to get organized. Thus, this errand she'd once looked forward to as a break from her fast-paced jobs had now become a joyless sojourn through hell. Indeed, she hadn't missed that ordeal during these past three days.

It helped her attitude, too, that Michael had turned out to be kinder than she'd expected. In fact, he'd been the one to ask the prince if she could retrieve her camera and other possessions. Also he'd been so gentle and compassionate when they'd been crammed in that horrible storage closet, and now, he seemed to be concerned about her every comfort.

As for Prince Abdul—she had to admit, she'd anticipated far worse. When Prince Abdul agreed to have her things returned, he'd appeared puzzled that they'd been confiscated. How ironic, she'd thought, that he'd held such loose reins with his servants, they were able to take such matters into their own hands without his knowledge. Nonetheless, even if now she'd begun to enjoy the adventure, she still felt aloof from the prince. He might be benevolent, but he remained a tyrant. Ordering Ishmael to abduct Michael and her remained inhumane and unusually cruel. Even if the prince required Ishmael to return her confiscated possessions, she remained angry. She had worried she wouldn't have her camera when she'd interview Isadora. Now, she had to buy more film and interview the model soon. She planned to slip away and find the room where the Goddess was staying in the prince's Beirut palace. If she saw Isadora and spoke with her, she would be able to decipher whether the model were abducted or whether she wanted to be here. Perhaps the woman would explain more about the gathering the prince had discussed. She wondered if the prince were a lunatic. Perhaps he was a religious fanatic, not merely a dedicated Moslem. *And who were those contractors? She must watch him more closely.*

Still, she tried to put those thoughts out of her mind by reading a few more bible verses, especially the psalms. Then she glanced at Scout, who lay on his side and snored on his corner of the bed. She slid off of it carefully so she wouldn't wake the dog, and slowly, she tiptoed to the window. The sun had already started to glare down on the city and rooftops, which twinkled under its light. From the fifth story, she could see over them and out to the bay. It beckoned her. Perhaps this prince who seemed so intent on appeasing them would accompany them on a shoreline outing. She glanced at her watch. It was only 8:15 a.m., and they'd dined until nearly eleven. Afterwards, the three of them had moved to a lounge where they sipped more drinks and watched couples dance. They didn't turn in until well after one. Still, she could sleep no longer and wanted to call Michael and urge him to escort her outside. She looked at the phone, at the alarm, and then again at her watch. No— it wouldn't be fair. Far too early. She'd have to go by herself. Besides,

Scout would be as good an escort, even if the dog wanted to continue sleeping right now. The sound of a door opening would bounce him to his feet.

The dog ran ahead and tugged on the lease, pulling Chelsey faster than she wanted to go. The two of them wove in and out of lines of palm trees on their way to the beach. Scout, of course, stopped at each tree, sniffed and marked his new territory. Meanwhile, Chelsey enjoyed inhaling air that carried saline smells from the Mediterranean.

She stopped to wait for the dog, when suddenly, she felt some cool, smooth fingers on the back of her neck. She flinched and whirled around. The prince stood there, grinning. He quickly withdrew the hand. Wearing jean shorts and an oversized T-shirt that sported a Nike logo, he stepped back, crossed a leg in front of an ankle, and tilted his head to one side, as if he posed for a snapshot. He cleared his throat. "Good morning, Miss McKay. You slept well, yes?"

She jumped and rubbed the back of her neck. "Yes, actually quite well." She looked at him awhile, studied his grin and the expression in his eyes. It'd changed somewhat from the night before, but she was unsure exactly how. Perhaps the sunlight made them less intense.

Today, his expression seemed more genuine. Perhaps, too, his casual dress was less imposing. She'd always believed an excess of ceremony revealed want of breeding, so she preferred this more laid-back approach—except for touching her neck. Then she looked down and adjusted the strap to her camera. She spoke without looking at him, and tried to keep her voice pleasant but somewhat flat. "How about you?"

He didn't answer but nodded toward the beach. "You want to visit the shoreline, yes?"

"Yes. Scout needs a run. And the sea looks inviting."

"May I accompany you?"

She squinted at him then shrugged. "Why not?"

Scout scampered up to them and sniffed Abdul's calves and knees. The prince squatted and patted the dog on the head, then rubbed his neck, and stroked his sides. "He is friendly. I have heard Dobermans are vicious."

She smiled. "Just don't try to attack me. And he's a miniature Doberman."

"I would never do that." He smiled and looked at the dog. Then he rubbed Scout's neck again, stood, and asked to take the dog's leash.

"That won't help," she said, but nonetheless, she handed it to him and smiled."

You like to banter, yes?"

She looked at him a moment then said, "Sometimes," then looked away and started walking toward the beach. She glanced back once to find him surveying her, so she turned away again and walked as gracefully as she could, walked, perhaps, like a princess.

Sea mist spraying their faces, the three of them ran along the shore later, darted around sunbathers and umbrellas, for perhaps an hour. Then they plopped on the sand at a spot near one of the docks and watched seagulls swoop and dive for fish, then soar so high they became tiny white commas, almost imperceptible in the clear blue sky. Sailboats glided across the sea, and their yellow and red-striped sails created a scene for a travel brochure. Smells of lamb and oil floated around them from a vendor selling falafel and gyro sandwiches on pita bread. For a *Globe* exclusive, Chelsey shot pictures of the boats, docks, and took one of the prince holding Scout on his lap. She could download these and send them to Greg this afternoon.

Then, Prince Abdul insisted he snap a photo of her, and later, he grabbed a passerby to shoot the three of them leaning against a dock. She was sure this was his mode of operation for a seductive routine, but today, she didn't chide him for it. She let herself enjoy this segue to information. *Why hadn't the prince revealed the true reason he'd brought them here?* Until he did, she couldn't trust him.

Further, she'd suffered enough the past two days. *What harm was there in having fun?* she wondered and decided to enjoy watching the prince pretend he was falling in love. She would be like Esther: She'd win his favor to help set her people free. Perhaps, too, to win her over, he'd lead her to Isadora. *That is, if the model were still in Beirut and if she were still alive.*

CHAPTER 25
The Press Forges On

All day, Jack had tried to reach his wife. It seemed she wouldn't answer the phone. He left messages each time, but he feared she was finally through with him. So he desperately wanted to get in touch with her. Nevertheless, he felt she was being unfair. He needed to be here. To stay home would've been shirking his duties—not only as an editor, but as the man who sent young Chelsey McKay into a city where political chaos ruled. He wasn't used to drinking so much, either, and by the afternoon, his head had started pounding. So while he and José cruised Beirut, first pursuing Ishmael el-Haddid, then staking out Prince Abdul's mansion, his temples hurt and his stomach was queasy. And after they picked up Fatima, his stomach grew worse, especially when he couldn't get through to his wife again.

"Shit. She'd got to be there," he said and turned off his phone, then slid it into his jacket. "I told her I'd call." He reached for his pipe and started to pack it.

"Why would she not wait for your call?" Fatima asked. She sat in the middle of the back seat and positioned her heels between the two men's seats. "Does she not want to talk with you? Did you offend her?"

"Yeah." The pipe in his mouth garbled his voice slightly, but without looking back at Fatima, he went on. "She's angry that I came here without her. But this isn't just a pleasure trip—I have business here, too."

"Really?" Fatima leaned forward till her head was over the compartment. "What is this business?"

"Newspapers."

"You sell newspapers? Like those boys on the street?"

"No." Jack glared at her. "I edit them. Uh, I edit one of them, you know, pull the entire thing together. Back in Nebraska—in the states."

"So what are you looking for here?"

"I'm doing a story."

"About what?"

Jack wrinkled his brow and turned around. "Why are you grilling me? Are you auditioning for a reporter's position or what?" He grinned.

"Grilling you? I thought grilling means cooking?"

Jack's first impulse was to call Fatima a smart-aleck, but then he realized she'd meant to be serious. "Why are you asking me so many questions?"

"I don't know." She shrugged. "I am sitting here in this car with two men I have never seen before. I think I should ask some questions."

"Hmmphf," Jack said and re-lit his pipe. "Maybe we should ask you how you know this Ishmael el-Haddid? What is *your* business?"

"That often varies." Fatima stared at the men, smiled slightly, and remained silent for a few minutes. Then, slowly, she added, "I am an honest working woman. This Ishmael offered to pay me for a job—my services, as you call them—and he has not. So I am here to collect my fee. He owes it to me, and he must pay me. I was very humiliated by the last job he sent me to do."

"Where did you meet Ishmael?" José asked. Up until then, he'd enjoyed the banter between the two others so much, he'd forgotten to interrogate Fatima.

"Oh, I saw him here and there." She twisted a strand of hair, then ran her fingers through it. "Around town. At bars and places."

"What other sort of places?"

"You know." She shrugged then leaned back in her seat and stared at the floor. "Restaurants. *Tourista* places."

"What sort of job did he hire you to do? Rob a bank?"

Fatima stiffened her back and leaned forward again. "Rob a bank? I told you I am an honest woman." She reached over and ran a thumb under José's lapel. "And what do you do? You edit newspapers, too?"

José drew back from her and nodded at his friend. "I work with Jack."

"You are not from Nebraska." She smiled. "I've seen you, I think."

"No." He grinned. He wanted to say, Virginia, but instead he added, "I live here."

She took her hand from his suit and shook it. "Then how do you know this man? This is too far to write for his paper!"

José frowned and squinted. "Haven't you heard of foreign correspondents? I've given Jack more than a few leads. And we were talking about you. How do you know this Ishmael? And what *specifically* did you do for him?"

She leaned back and put her face in her hands. "Who are *you* really? Why are you asking me these questions? You are treating me as if I were a criminal—a robber or something. I am not."

"Look, we don't mean any harm to you." Jack said in a softer voice. "We just want to find out more about this Ishmael. You know about the bombings?"

"Bombings? Where?"

"Here in Beirut," José said. "Two American fast-food places."

"When?"

"Yesterday," José said. "We think maybe Ishmael might know someone involved. He might have been involved. We want the story."

She dropped her hands to her lap and shook her head. "No. I don't think so. Ishmael works for Prince Abdul El Fashid from Saudi Arabia. It would do him no good to bomb American businesses. The prince has contracts with many of them. He may be crazy but not that crazy."

Jack turned to look at her. "You seem to know a lot about him. What does Ishmael do for the prince?"

"Lots of things. Like now, he's been driving around two Americans—a man and a woman. I think the prince has contracts with them or something. Last night, they ate dinner together at the Portemilio, the big hotel near the beach."

"Did you see the Americans?" Jack asked.

"Oh yes." Fatima smiled. "The woman—or I should say, girl—is very nice. And she has hair like the sun. Very lovely" Her chest swelled. "She asked me to eat dinner with them."

"Where are the Americans staying—in the palace?"

"I don't know." She smiled. "They might be at the Hotel Portemilio. That is where Prince Abdul El Fashid entertains his guests. Especially his pretty women guests."

CHAPTER 26
Michael Investigates

For the first time in fifteen years, Michael Levine slept in. The windows in his room faced west, and the eastern sun didn't wake him as it had Chelsey. So he didn't open his eyes until well after ten, and when he did, he groaned. His back and legs ached, his sinuses and throat felt parched, and his stomach growled. He felt he smelled like a stable housing horses ready to be sent to glue factories. When he stumbled to the mirror, he observed puffy eyes with deep creases and dark circles under them. "Huh!" he said aloud. "I look better when I don't get a good night's sleep."

After splashing his face with water, swishing mouthwash, running a toothbrush over his tongue, and clicking on the coffee, he moved to the window and drew up the shade. *It'll be another hot one*, he thought. *At least, with Ishmael out of the way, I can get something done.* Indeed, this was the opportunity he'd been waiting for since long before Isadora's disappearance.

It'd been a long time since he'd worked as an investigative reporter. But he still had the instincts. Indeed, he'd liked that work far more than the advertising positions he'd switched to so he could make more cash.

And more benefits. Yes, the sales rep jobs boosted him up the ladder to the publisher slot, where he now rested comfortably. Almost. He missed covering stories, getting the inside scoop before even editors knew what was happening. Now, it seemed the advertisers called almost all the shots. And his business was to please them. So when he heard of some interesting underhanded scheme, similar to the Enron scam or the WorldCom plot, he had to ignore it. This disturbed his reporting soul, but on the other hand, his jobs paid well. After a few years, he'd resigned himself to this fate and made the best of it. Besides, he reassured himself, someday, when he retired, he'd write novels about the sort of intrigues he couldn't expose now. Plus, with the connections he'd made the past twenty years, he'd likely release some good, strong sellers and live off advances and royalties.

And now, he'd stumbled into one, huge international story—and Isadora's disappearance was fair game. It'd hurt none of his advertisers—the big fashion houses—if he unearthed the conspiracies connected with her disappearance. Because El Fashid wouldn't—or perhaps, *truly couldn't*—talk without losing his life, Michael was sure this scheme involved some anti-American Arab underground, some group comprising fundamentalist terrorists, akin to the Al-Qaeda at the turn of the century. Osama bin Laden's followers still bombed embassies and hijacked planes, even after their leader died. It seemed they were nearly as active now as during the U.S. wars in Iraq and in

Afghanistan. Maybe another fringe group had contracted the prince to bring her to it. Many times, Isadora had been vulnerable, especially to sweet-talking men. Because the prince romanced her and paid her well, she may have likely joined him here of her own accord. Still, Michael worried about El Fashid's plans for her, him, and Chelsey.

***

What did Arab fundamentalists want with us? Michael asked himself over and over. He wondered what they planned to do with them. Would they use them to set an example to the western world, as they'd hoped to do with their other slaughters? Perhaps Chelsey was onto something. Perhaps the wacky prince had joined a cult that planned to sacrifice everyone. These recurring thoughts sent Michael's mind racing, so he swallowed but two sips of coffee, skipped his aerobics, and hurriedly slid on trousers and a shirt, then rushed down a fire exit, where he took steps two at a time.

The prince's loose reins would give him a chance to find Isadora. But he wasn't sure how to locate the Beirut palace. Under flickering palms and the bluest sky he'd seen in a long time, he wandered toward the shoreline, where he'd check with a shop-owner about the palace's whereabouts. If he was lucky, one of the locals would know about it. As he strode closer the beach, he heard, among the rumbling sounds of tourists, a familiar voice. It was Chelsey's. He turned toward the voice, which came from about a hundred feet away. There, along the shore,

Chelsey, the prince, and her dog frolicked, stepping in and out of the incoming tide. They hadn't seen him, and he debated whether to acknowledge them.

He decided to watch them awhile. Moving into the fringe of a crowd of tourists, he almost ran head-on into a man clicking snapshots. Michael ducked his camera and maneuvered his way through the throngs to a spot where he could watch the couple. *Although they appeared to focus on the dog, which scampered unleashed now between them, some strong chemistry sparked there, too*, he thought. They'd brush each other's hands when they'd stop to pat the dog, look at each other for more than the obligatory thirty seconds, and they laughed repeatedly. The prince brushed something off Chelsey's forehead, and she didn't flinch. In fact, she smiled. Apparently, she no longer saw him as a chauvinist, or if she did, she hid the feelings well.

Michael worried about her. *How savvy she was she really? What if this prince succeeded at seducing her? What then? Would it help or hurt them and their insane mission to bring Isadora home?* "Hmmm?" he said aloud. He wasn't sure Isadora wanted to leave this place. And the prince was likely applying the techniques he'd used on the model to Chelsey. He might persuade Chelsey to stay, too. For now, he could do nothing, but he made a mental note to discuss this with her as soon as he could. Now, the prince's appearance foiled his plans. If he made an attempt to learn anything about the palace, a shop-owner would likely have spotted the prince, too. Then, when Michael asked about the palace nearby, the vendor would merely point out the prince instead of providing background about the building, which Michael needed to learn.

So he turned away from the coast and headed back toward town. He'd have to try to call Jack. Michael was sure Jack's CIA buddy was stationed here. Besides, it wouldn't hurt to let Jack know he and Chelsey were still alive. He made his way up the hill, found a palm out-of-sight from the shore, and punched out Jack's number. After what seemed like an eternity, the line connected. It was busy, of course. He tried again and waited for the long connection. Too soon—still busy. Then, from seemingly out of nowhere, a large, green and yellow parrot flew onto Michael's right shoulder. It flapped its wings, squawked, and dug its nails into his shirt.

Awed, Michael didn't know what to do. He glanced around for some owner who chased the bird. He saw no one. He spoke softly to the parrot, cooed to it, and tried to see it if would fly off or step down to his biceps, then forearm, where he might be able to shake it off without hurting either of them. But it was comfortably perched. Squawking again, it dug its claws in deeper. Michael felt them press through his shirt. Now, he didn't dare to swat at it or to pick it up with his left hand because the bird would likely dig its claws in deeper, tear the shirt and probably his flesh, too. Or the bird might empty its bowels on his shirt.

He ran a finger across the tips of the bird's wings. Surely, they'd been clipped. With its red markings, it had to be one of those Amazon parrots. Expensive, too. Certainly, its owner was desperate to find it. But he still saw no one looking for something. He decided to walk back toward the crowds. Obviously, some local knew who owned the feathered beast. Meanwhile, he continued cooing to keep the bird from digging in deeper. So the two of them loped back down the hill, with Michael bouncing his steps in hopes of dislodging the bird or encouraging it to fly to a more congenial host. For some reason, the parrot remained attached to Michael's shoulder and wouldn't move from its perch. And every few minutes, the bird would squawk.

As they loped along, a young American-looking girl and boy joined them. The girl giggled and clapped her hands while the boy pointed to the bird, then waved a hand in front of it. Michael hoped this would shoo it away, but instead, the bird dug its nails in even deeper. Finally, Michael asked them to stop, it'd make the bird angry and it might claw them, he warned. Meanwhile, a woman called their names and the children ran to her, remarking, "Momma, the man has a giant bird for a pet. Come see it!" Fortunately, the woman had better sense than to follow this unwilling Pied Piper, so Michael was able to slip away. He decided someone at the bar might know the parrot's owner. If not, he'd sell the bird to someone there.

He opened the door to a dark bar, when suddenly, he heard a young woman's voice call his name. Instinctively, he swung around and saw Chelsey and the prince rushing toward him. He sighed. Today, nothing had gone according to plan. Remarking to himself that he needed to talk with Chelsey anyway, before she became too enamored with the prince, he forced a smile.

"Where'd you get this?" Chelsey remarked and began cooing to the bird. She stroked its back. The parrot didn't seem to mind. It lowered its head, much in the manner a cat would when someone petted it.

Michael shrugged the best he could with a parrot on his right shoulder. "It just flew in and landed. And its claws are starting to hurt."

Chelsey laughed and so did the prince, who came up beside her.

"That is a very valuable bird," he said.

"I know. But I can't find its owner. I thought I'd check with the bartender here."

So the three of them entered the bar and sat at a table. As it turned out, the parrot belonged to one of the shopkeepers, whom the bartender knew. The parrot still wouldn't budge, so Michael found directions to the owner's shop. By then, it was after 11:30, so Chelsey and the prince wanted to stay for lunch and asked Michael to join them. His plans had run so awry by now, he agreed to return after he dropped off the parrot. He rushed to the shop, where the owner was so glad to see his pet that he paid Michael the equivalent of fifty U.S. dollars. So relieved to have the bird detached from his shoulder, Michael hurried out, brushed some feather barbs off his shoulder, and rushed back to bar. By the time he joined Chelsey and the prince, he'd forgotten to try Jack's number again. Another day in this strange paradise had turned his schedule upside-down, much like a parrot swinging under a post.

CHAPTER 27
Time to Split

José and Jack were uncertain whether they should stake-out the palace or the hotel. They sat in the van, with Fatima still in tow, and discussed whether or not to split up.

"I could hail a cab," Jack suggested and struck a match on his zipper. He re-lit his pipe, which seemed to go out more quickly in the hot, dry climate. "Then I'll wait in the Portemilio's lobby and see what happens."

"But you aren't carrying." José frowned and studied Jack awhile. Since he'd seen him ten years before, the newspaperman had gained at least fifty pounds, and the way he'd seen Jack drinking and smoking, José worried his friend could neither run very fast, if at all, nor defend himself against an anemic insect. "What if that thug Ishmael's still hovering over them? What would you do?"

Jack sighed. "At least, we'd know where they are." He nodded at Fatima. "And if she's right, they may never show up here. We'd be just wasting time. Besides, Ishmael may recognize this car. Didn't take him long to lose us."

"Yeah." José patted the steering. "She ain't for high-speed chases."

Jack laughed. "We weren't going fast."

"Well, she ain't too good on sharp corners, either." José frowned and turned toward Fatima, who now sat further back. With the insides of her purse spread out across the seat, she was filing a chipped nail. "What do you think, Ma'am? You mind staying alone with me here while he grabs a cab?"

She glared at him a minute. "I don't know. You still haven't told me who you are."

José shrugged. "Your choice. You can wait in the blistering sun— or stay in here. Frankly, I don't care."

Just as Fatima opened the door and had poked out a leg, the limo swung around a corner into the drive. She smiled. "Here he is anyway." Sliding across the seat and onto the pavement, she snagged one of her stockings on the door rim. "Shit! Another run!" She frowned, spun around and smoothed the side of her leg where the run in the stocking had started.

The two men disembarked, too, but lagged behind Fatima. She hurried toward the limo, then sprinted in front of it and waved her hands, as if she were an airport ground controller.

The limo screeched but stopped before hitting her. Ishmael flung open the door. "What are you doing here?" he thundered.

"I want my money, you cur!" Fatima stopped flailing her arms and stomped over to Ishmael. She swung her purse at him, missed his face but cuffed one of his ears. "And I want it now!" He ducked and backed away from her. But once he caught his balance, he crossed his arms and puffed out his chest.

A few yards behind, still hidden by foliage, José and Jack stifled their chuckles.

"You've got to admit, she's got spunk," Jack said. "You ought to hire her."

"That whore?" José replied. "She'd likely turn our men against us."

"I dunno." Jack chewed on his pipe. "Pay her well, and she might turn out to be your best agent. I can't believe she's so gutsy around an armed man."

Fatima's face had grown red now. She wasn't taking excuses. "You have shamed me!" she shrieked. "In fact, Mr. Ishmael, because I left the hotel in disgrace when I was only doing my job, you pay me double!"

Ishmael squinted, drew in a breath and sighed deeply. "Okay, okay." He drew out a large roll from his pants' pocket and thumbed off several hundred riyals.

"No—you said double—I will not take less!"

"This is double." Ishmael frowned.

Fatima stared at him and crossed her arms. "Liar!"

Ishmael sighed again. He glanced at the van that had housed José and Jack and noticed the two men were no longer there. Ishmael then unpeeled more bills. With the way things had turned out, he didn't believe he should pay her anything. But he wondered if she had gone to the police. He was sure he'd seen the van and dark-haired man around town. He needed no policeman interrogating him.

He also figured Fatima might come in handy for other jobs, maybe entertaining some more of the prince's clients. Many of them had requested her by name. Perhaps he'd use her again with the prince, too, who, after all, hadn't kicked her out of the Portemilio. Maybe the prince liked her better than the others Ishmael had sent him. And today, he knew the Americans were influencing the prince too much. He didn't like the way the prince allowed Chelsey to do what she wanted. He feared the prince was becoming enamored with her. Yes, Fatima may be valuable another day soon, so he paid up.

Meanwhile, the two men in the bushes still debated what to do next. Obviously, neither Chelsey nor Michael were in the limo. They considered that it could be some time before another vehicle would come or leave the palace. And at least, in the Portemilio's lobby, they'd fit into the crowd. Besides, José added, he could put another agent near this gate. So the two drove off toward the hotel near the Beirut shoreline.

CHAPTER 28
Michael Investigates Again

After the threesome had finished lunch and the prince had gone to the register to pay for the meal, Michael drew Chelsey outside. Scout followed them, and Chelsey spread out a napkin that contained table scraps for the dog. He gobbled them.

"You seem to like him." Michael nodded at the restaurant. He held two mints, offered her one, unwrapped the other, and popped it into his mouth. "Maybe too much?"

"Don't be silly." Chelsey smiled and winked. "I trust him even less than I trust you."

"Really?" Michael crunched on the mint. "Me? Who tried to help you escape?"

She shrugged. "Maybe that was part of this pageant. Maybe you're in on this escapade, too." She turned from him and stared at a group of palms that edged the restaurant's grounds. Two gulls soared over them and headed toward the bay. Still hot, the temperature felt far more comfortable than it did during most Midwestern Augusts. Chelsey had noticed she hadn't sweated much since she'd arrived. She sweated heavily through Nebraska summers, *she always did*. At least here, she felt relieved not to have to change her blouse each time she came in from outside, relieved not to worry about her hair drooping or frizzing, relieved not to worry about her makeup running.

Michael chuckled. "If I were, believe me, I'd never have put up with Ishmael."

She looked back at him. "I'm sorry. I don't know what to believe anymore. The prince asked me to stay in his Beirut palace again. I don't know if we'd be better off there or here. I don't want to sleep with him, but I'm afraid that's the only way I might get him to tell me what's going on."

"Keep your distance, Missy." Michael swallowed the remnants of the mint and poked at his gums with a toothpick. "Sleeping with him won't get you anywhere. Always remember—men are pigs."

Chelsey smiled broadly. "Spoken by a true oinker."

"You might be right." He patted her on the back then drew her into a hug. "We're all jerks, aren't we?"

Abdul stepped outside in time to see Michael hugging Chelsey. He frowned and looked down at the bushes edging the restaurant lot. In his hand, he clasped mints he'd brought for Chelsey. She saw him over Michael's shoulders, drew back from Levine, and said, "Hey! We've been waiting for you."

He smiled stiffly, then reached out and dropped chocolate-covered mints into her hand. Then, he tossed Scout a bone.

"I'd like to walk by myself for awhile. Go through the area around the hotel, maybe see some of the galleries there. If you don't mind," Michael said and looked up the hill. He grinned. "I promise I'll return."

"Yes. I want you to enjoy this lovely city." The prince grinned back. "And if you get lost, you know Ishmael will find you."

"Yeah." Michael smirked, turned away and began strolling to where he was when the parrot had befriended him. When he'd gone far enough to be out of their sight, he tried dialing Jack again. This time, he made it through to *The Globe*. But static interfered with the connection. Nonetheless, whoever answered heard him.

"Jack? He's out-of-town. He's in—" The static flared up again, and Michael couldn't hear where he was.

"Where?" he asked. Again, the person gave a name and the static muffled his words.

"Can't hear you. Too much static. Where?" Michael was shouting now, and he felt more frustrated each time the static flared.

"He's in—" The connection cut out completely. Michael tried punching in the number again, but this time, he couldn't get through. He turned off the phone and put it back in his pocket. Maybe the hotel phones would work better. He'd try a pay phone there. The prince's mention of galleries gave him an idea: He'd check there to find the location of the palace. Before either he or Chelsey relocated, he'd talk to Isadora, get the scoop on what was really going on.

Finally, Michael ran into some luck. The second gallery owner had sold many paintings to the prince. After Michael showed him his press-card, he gave him the address. So he hailed a taxi and within fifteen minutes arrived not far the palace gates. He asked the driver to drop him off; he'd walk the rest of the way.

Later, when Chelsey and the prince walked the dog back to the Portimelio, she noticed a light green Dodge Caravan with two men in it in the distance. The van turned onto the street in front of the hotel. For some reason, it caught her attention, perhaps, she reflected, because she hadn't seen such a vehicle since she'd arrived in the city. Even if many old models of American cars abounded here, that one seemed out-of-place. From across the grounds, she watched the two men slip out of the van and saunter into the lobby. Something about one of them, his gate, his hair—she was unsure—seemed familiar. Then she shrugged at the thought. She knew only three men in Beirut, and none of them would ride in such a hideous van, the color of day-old, split-pea soup. *Apparently, they're American tourists with little money and poor taste,* she reflected. *That's probably all there is to it.*

CHAPTER 29
Eleventh Heaven

Even though Liwet and Dardiel worked nine hours a day transforming the laboratory, strip by strip, into a luxurious cruise ship, it seemed that too much work still remained only four days before take-off. Liwet had worked so hard, his feathers had become frayed, he felt frazzled, and now, he slumped in a corner under one of the computer centers.

"I know I'm showing lack of faith," he said, then sighed, brought his fingers to his mouth, and began chewing the tips of his short nails. "But I just don't see how we can make it on time. Look at these walls. They are only half-way completed!"

"Faith is the opposite of evidence," Dardiel replied. "And you, like many of the *homo sapiens*, rely too much upon proof to build your faith. It does not work that way. We must believe first—then we receive."

"What's your secret to keeping your faith?"

"It is not a secret." Dardiel sighed and his eye sockets drooped. "It is in the guidebook. I fear, my friend, you have been lax in your reading."

Liwet reddened. "Yes. With this added work, I've fallen behind."

"Ah, but the guidebook will help you work faster, my friend." Dardiel smiled, swooped over to Liwet, and he gently patted his colleague's head. "You see, faith relies upon the unseen. It is our vision. We must act as if what is not yet seen has already come to pass. Look at the earthlings gathering below. Our faith has drawn such unlikely ones together—and soon, they will enter this ship and spend an eternity together. Who would have thought this reality would have come to pass, except those who read the guidebook?"

"You are right, as usual." Liwet sighed then drew himself up from the floor. "Frankly, I'm amazed at how quickly Chelsey has grown fond of the prince." His squeaky voice grew higher and lighter. "Yes, that illustrates faith. We saw them coming together long before they realized it themselves." He flew around the room, up to the ceiling and back down. "I see it almost finished, even completed now. Oh, you are so wise."

Dardiel smiled. "But remember, even I doubted whether Mr. Levine should be on the list. I, too, had been weak. I had become lax about my reading then. See, what happened after I returned to it? Everything is planned. We must follow that plan, and each piece will fall into place at its allotted time. Who knows, perhaps I will gain more faith in the earthlings—those crazy *homo sapiens*—after all."

Liwet clicked his wings together and fluttered back to where his friend worked. He sighed and looked toward the planet earth. "Now, that indeed will take much faith. I would have said more than I can muster right now, but I have been watching that Prince Abdul El Fashid. He seemed to have become a changed man. He seems to be operating upon the force of love—not that cheap lust and greed, traits that have kept him hovering too near the earth. This earthling-watching has become far more interesting the past few days. "

CHAPTER 30
Making Plans

After they shared the day playing with Scout along the shore, the prince appeared outside Chelsey's room the next morning. And he appeared every morning for the next five days. He'd taken leave from work, so each morning, he'd knock and say hello before she'd made plans. And each day, they'd spend afternoons strolling in and out of shops and galleries. He hadn't returned to the palace since, either. One evening, he left for half an hour and returned with a gift.

"Open it," he said. "You will find my secrets."

Carefully, she pulled tape from the edges of the gold foil paper— so pretty, she wanted to save it. Inside, she saw a small poetry book with a man and woman on the cover. It was Pablo Neruda's *Twenty Love Poems and a Song of Despair*. "Thank you. I miss reading poetry." She smiled and flipped through the pages. "I haven't had time to read much of it since I started with *The Globe*."

Abdul sat down in the chair beside her and crossed his legs. "Now, you do."

She stopped at a page. "Well, look at this. In 'Girl Lithe and Tawny,' he uses 'dark butterfly.' Hmmm."

The prince smiled. "I told you. This book contains my secrets. But for you, I want to write my own words. And we can share Neruda's words each night, too, if you like."

"That sounds pleasant." Then she knit her eyebrows and squinted. "But how long will we stay here?"

"Would you prefer to stay in the palace?"

"Only if I can talk to Isadora."

The prince stared at her a few seconds. "Of course, you can. Why did you not ask me before?"

"I thought you didn't want me talking with her."

The prince laughed. "I did not say that. At first, I worried."

"No. But isn't that why you had Ishmael abduct us?"

He sighed heavily, stood, and moved over to her. "No. I was told to bring you here."

"By whom? Terrorists?"

Prince Abdul chuckled. "Oh, no."

"Then who are these people? What do they want with us?"

"I cannot tell you that."

"Why not?"

"Because I do not know what the final plan will be."

"What? This makes *no* sense. What power do they have over you?"

The prince sighed again and turned away from her, went to the window, and stared into the sky. The palm trees swayed in the wind, and a few clouds had popped up on the horizon. "I do not know that, either. But they are more powerful than you can imagine." He stopped for a moment, looked back at Chelsey and sighed. "Please do not think I am crazy. But these contractors are different. They are not human beings."

"What?"

"I am serious." He looked into the night sky.

She moved over to the window and stood beside him. "And what are you looking at?"

"You see that planet, which looks like a star, just rising over the horizon? You see how bright it is?"

"Yes." She crossed her arms. "You're changing the subject."

"No. I am not. Please listen while I try to answer you." He reached out and squeezed one of her hands. "And please do not think I am crazy."

"Well, you seem a bit crazy for bringing us here without a reason." She smiled slightly. "But otherwise, you seem sane."

"This will sound strange, but it is true. The beings—for again, they are not humans—they are greater than us, more powerful—with skin so translucent, it glimmers like those stars. They who have asked me to bring you here are from another place, another universe perhaps."

She stared at him without speaking. She blinked and shook her head. *This was insane. Yes, he certainly was a member of some cult, much like the Heaven's Gate cult.* She would be sure to not take any more liquids from him. Suddenly, she withdrew her hand, moved to the couch, and sat down. "You're telling me that some aliens had you abduct me and Michael? And you expect me to believe you?"

When the prince whirled around and faced her, tears filled his eyes. He shook his head. "I warned you. You see why I could not tell you this?" He lifted his hands as if he were praying. "I understand how unbelievable this sounds. But I am not lying. And at least, about this, I am not crazy. These beings exist—and they command powers in the universe that we cannot perceive. They stopped my jet a few months ago, and yet, it did not fall from the sky. They came into the cabin and gave me a list. Your name was on it. So was Michael's."

For a long time, she stared at the coffee table, then began running a forefinger around the edge of a vase holding orchids. At last, she looked back at him. "So when do we meet these creatures?"

"In just a few days."

"They're coming here?"

He shook his head. "No. We must meet them elsewhere."

"Where?" "Jerusalem."

Chelsey leaned back on the couch. Now, tears filled her eyes, too. "I must talk with Isadora," she said. "Very soon."

The prince stared at her then reached over and stroked the back of one of her hands. "Now that I know you better, Chelsey, I see how wrong I was to order Ishmael to bring you here." He looked down at her fingers, then slid his other hand underneath hers and squeezed it gently between his two palms. "In fact, after you talk with Isadora, which I can arrange immediately, you are free to leave here. You are free to leave Lebanon, if that is what you desire. I will not keep you caged any longer."

She looked into his eyes and nodded. "Thank you," she said and blinked away more tears. She looked away from him awhile, then looked back and smiled. She'd begun to like him, but indeed, the man was loony.

***

At that moment, the prince decided he would dedicate his latest poem to Miss Chelsey McKay, whether she wanted him to do so or not. And whether she liked him or not, she would listen to these words, at least, he hoped.

CHAPTER 31
Meeting Isadora

Chelsey was awed by the Goddess. *No wonder they call her that*, she thought. The model's face was as smooth as if it were chiseled from granite. Even if she were slightly older than she appeared in her photos, she was unlike most models, who often appear far more glamorous in magazines than in real life. Indeed, Isadora glowed with a charisma that no camera could capture completely. When Chelsey walked in with Abdul, the Goddess swished across the room, stretched out her arms and at once, embraced both of them in a hug. "I've been dying to meet you," she said to Chelsey. "Prince Abdul has talked about you every day." Her voice, light and lilting, flowed as smoothly as honey over toast, and Chelsey's knees nearly quivered.

The woman seemed as if she were from a different universe. This was the closest she'd been to the model. She'd seen her only twice before, and both times, it was from a distance. Ten years ago, Neil had brought her to a fashion show in Kansas City that the ad agency he worked for sponsored. So from a press room perhaps fifty yards away, Chelsey had first seen the tall, sleek model move briskly down a runway a few times. And Chelsey had been too young then to remember much, except the tall model's beautiful golden hair, long, flowing gowns and lively gait. Those images, especially the golden hair, had remained.

Two days ago, Michael had told her Isadora suffered from some obscure heart problem, a value that leaked, but Chelsey believed it was something else. She perceived that the frail model was epileptic. The second time she'd seen the Goddess, six years later, had been in New York at an after-show party. The waiters had popped champagne bottles, filled glasses until the bubbly overflowed, and passed them around to everyone, even Chelsey, who was underage. She drank only one glass, but it sent her head buzzing. Then an hour or so later, three or four men carried a swooned Isadora outside. Chelsey joined the crowd that followed. "Is she all right?" someone asked. Another said, "Yes—she just needs air." A man whom Chelsey assumed was Isadora's date, positioned the Goddess on her back across the hood of a Corvette. She went into convulsions, rocked her pelvis back and forth, then up and down, as if she were making love to the air. Chelsey had been running toward her, but when she saw that, she stopped half-way across the lawn, frightened, and asked if someone had called an ambulance.

She was sure Isadora was experiencing an epileptic seizure. No one else seemed very concerned. After the model quit moving and fell into another swoon, her date scooped her up, placed her in the front seat of his car, and drove away. She'd never learned where they went or what exactly had happened. Some of the persons had said, no, Isadora was not an epileptic. That image had also haunted Chelsey.

Today, Chelsey watched the Goddess intently. Now Isadora certainly showed no traces of ill health. And she appeared to be genuinely happy. After hugging Michael and Chelsey, she stepped back as if to admire the couple. "And he told me you were pretty, but not *this* pretty." The model smiled, winked and hugged Chelsey again.

"I'm hardly a model." Chelsey reddened and looked at the floor. It was black marble with thin white streaks. A huge, scarlet and gold oriental carpet covered most of it, but a large portion of the floor was left bare, *to show off the marble, no doubt.* Then, she glanced around the room. The prince had given Isadora one of the finest and largest. It was similar to an exclusive apartment in the upper East Eighties. Crown molding with an ornate, leafy trim edged mauve walls that stretched to at least twelve feet. Huge windows covered one side of the room. Beneath it was a carved window-seat. A chandelier hung in the living room area, and someone had left the bedroom door ajar, so Chelsey could see that room was nearly as large as this parlor. She looked back at Isadora and smiled weakly. "I'm too short."

The Goddess raised her eyebrows. "You're lucky, you see. You are able to use your mind to make money. A model's life isn't as glamorous as it seems." She lifted an arm and waved it over a couch. "Please, take a seat. I'll have the maid bring us tea, baklava, crumpets—or if you prefer, pita bread." She laughed. "Yes, now I can eat what I like—don't have to stick to celery, egg whites, broth, diet pills, and cocaine."

Chelsey blinked. *No wonder Isadora didn't want to leave*, she thought as she and Abdul took a seat on the couch. The model moved to the huge window and drew the shutters half-way closed to soften the glare, then turned and sat upon a chair near the two others. "I understand you want to interview me." She smiled broadly. "But I'm unsure why."

"Most of the world believes you've been kidnapped," Chelsey said. "Of course, everyone wonders who did it and why."

Isadora smiled even more broadly, as if posing on a *Vogue* cover for a sunny, spring issue. "As if I didn't have the gumption to simply walk out?"

Abdul knit his eyebrows. "Come on, Isadora. If you would have told someone, no one would have worried."

She blinked. "I did. I told Michael I came here of my own accord— that I'm happy for the first time in my life and don't want to leave." She looked from the prince to Chelsey. "Didn't he tell you?"

"Well, Yes. And no." Chelsey frowned. "He said you came here at the prince's invitation. But he wasn't sure if you'd been drugged or otherwise coerced."

The Goddess tossed back her head, her long waves of hair flying, and laughed loudly. "He didn't believe me! After all these years!" Then she looked at Chelsey, raised her arms, and ran her fingers across her veins, still prominent in her thin arms. She smiled broadly. "Look. For the first time since just after I started modeling, I'm not using drugs."

Chelsey noted that no track marks ran up her arms and wondered if once they had. "I believe you." She looked down, twisted one of her ringlets, then looked back at the model. "He also said something about a trip. Are you going to Jerusalem?"

She nodded. "And the rest of the way, too."

Chelsey looked at her a few seconds then stared at the plaster ceiling. She pictured an awful scene: Images of the Heaven's Gate webmasters in body bags after they'd poisoned themselves, believing a spaceship would pick up their souls, flashed through her mind. And then, there was the Solar Temple cult in the Canary Islands. Had Spanish policemen not foiled that group's suicide plot, more than thirty people would have killed themselves on top of Tenerife's Teide volcano. *Was the prince planning to gather a following together for a mass suicide?* she wondered.

He *had* coerced her to come here. On the other hand, he'd said nothing about an apocalypse. And after he'd revealed why he'd brought her here and what the plans were, he'd told her she could go free. So Chelsey wasn't sure what to think about this upcoming Jerusalem trip. "What do you mean?" she asked.

Isadora wrinkled her brow, frowned, and looked at the prince. He shrugged. She looked back at Chelsey. "The trip into the heavens, into a new world—a new Heaven, another universe. You know about that, don't you? Or didn't Abdul tell you about the beings and the mission?"

"I wanted to make sure we were on the same page." She looked from Isadora to the prince. "And I want to know what we are supposed to do in Jerusalem. Climb a mountain and take cyanide?"

"I hope not!" The prince's face grew pale. Now he worried. The beings had said nothing to him about suicide. *Surely, they'd not planned to kill the people he brought to them or coerce them to kill themselves— or did they?* He worried that perhaps, after all, the beings were evil *jinn* who'd tricked him. He leaned forward and cupped his face in his hands. He said nothing more but stood, ambled to the window, and looked at the western sky. The sun had just dropped below the horizon, leaving red and gold streaks in its wake. A line of purple clouds cut through them. He stared intensely, then closed his eyes and sent out a thought— or perhaps a prayer—to those beings who'd visited him. He decided right then that unless they clarified this situation, he wouldn't bring anyone to him, no matter how much money they offered.

On the way back from the palace, Chelsey and the prince rode in the back of the limo without speaking awhile. Then Chelsey pressed one of her palms on top of the back of his. "Listen. After we get home, could I have about an hour by myself?"

The prince blinked. "Of course. We are still sharing dinner, yes?"

She nodded. "Sure. I'm famished."

After he walked her to her room and she'd locked the door behind him, Chelsey patted Scout on the head. She didn't take time to play with him, though, because she immediately started packing. The chore would be harder now, she realized, after she dug out her two suitcases. The prince's generosity had expanded her wardrobe dramatically. Of course, she could leave the dresses Madame Loiselle had fashioned. But she didn't feel quite right about doing that. Even if she couldn't go along with the crazy scheme, she'd grown fond of Abdul. *Perhaps I could pick up the second bag tomorrow*, she thought. Then she'd need to pack only one suitcase. On the other hand, perhaps by then, the prince would change his mind. So she'd have to act fast. Suddenly, she remembered she had to phone Michael. He had no idea they were free to leave. She rang his room. No answer. She tried again and left a message.

As she crammed in pumps, stockings, knee socks, and sandals, she came across a shell the prince had discovered and given her. Inside, the bluish pearl covering looked so much like the sky that day, she remembered the two of them running on the shore with Scout. *It didn't matter*, she told herself. *He'd only been trying to seduce me into staying so he could turn me over to the aliens, if they even existed. Perhaps the man is just nuts—probably a result of too much inbreeding.* Then, she reconsidered the thought. *With their multiple wives, the Arabs probably suffered far less from inbreeding than western nobility.* She chuckled softly at that. Nonetheless, she had to leave this insane situation. She sighed and squeezed the sandals into a side pocket. Then she spread out her garment bag upon the bed. She had extra hangers, so perhaps taking the extra three dresses wouldn't be such a problem after all.

When she turned back to the closet to unhook one of the gowns, a strong white light flooded the room. Wondering if someone had aimed a huge spotlight at the building, she glanced at the window. Perhaps the prince had changed his mind already and ordered someone—most likely the detestable Ishmael—to guard her. But the light didn't come from her window.

She moved to the doorway connecting her bed room to the parlor and looked at the picture window. No light there. Then she glanced the other way and saw a tall being radiating the light—the intense, white light that made her squint. She drew up a hand to shelter her eyes. Boldly, she straightened and walked toward the being, who now had his back to her. His wings flickered a minute and he whirled around, almost clipping her with a wing. "Hello, Miss—or I should say, Ms. I have not yet adapted to this new custom—Ms. McKay." His squeaky voice made her ears ring.

Chelsey stepped back, even though she found it difficult to move with her knees quivering so wildly. Awed, she stepped further back and dropped into a chair. "My God, it's true."

"No. I am not He." The being chuckled. He fluttered his wings, and bits of feathers scattered around him. He brushed them away with one of his feet. "I am merely Gabriel. His light would blind your eyes."

Chelsey reddened. "Only an expression."

"Not taking the name in vain, I hope?"

"No—o. I mean, I'm just . . . just flabbergasted." She drew up her arms and opened her palms toward him, as if she asked a question.

"Why?" Gabriel folded his wings behind him. "You read the guidebook almost every day." Then, his wings fluttered slightly. "Do you think those are just legends? Fairy stories for children?"

Chelsey shook her head. Her mouth gaped. "I don't know. I—"

"Take my word for it, they are not. Neither is the prince lying."

"Then, then what *do* you want with us?"

"You have been called. You have been chosen."

"For what?"

"I believe you know. Re-read the guidebook. The last few sections."

Mouth still gaping, Chelsey blinked, then she closed her eyes for a few seconds. And when she opened them, Gabriel was gone.

That was it, she thought, she simply had to catch up on her sleep. Now, she was hallucinating. For surely, this had been a hallucination, no matter how real. If she lost more sleep, who could tell what would happen next? As if in a dream, she meandered back to the bed room and sat on the bed. She drew her hands to her temples. How had that image (or whatever it was) entered her suite? She could have dismissed it as a hologram except the thing spoke, too. Then she wondered if someone had set up a movie projector to set up the phantasmagoria in her room. Perhaps the prince had a staff member set up this display so she would go along with his plans. That was it—it was all just a put-up job. A set-up to make her look like a fool.

She glanced at her bags in the closet. She pulled blouses and T-shirts from hangers and stuffed them into bags. She cleared out drawers. Yes, she decided to continue packing—it wouldn't matter if she left for Jerusalem or for Nebraska. Either way, she'd leave Beirut soon. But was the only certainty she held about her future.

CHAPTER 32
Connecting

Although for four days, CIA agents took turns monitoring the prince's palace, none of them spotted anyone other than Ishmael, maids, gardeners, and other staff workers enter and exit the building or leave the grounds. In fact, they found it odd that Prince Abdul El Fashid never passed through the gates, either. Other agents outside the prince's office also hadn't seen him come or go. So José called off the stake-out. He and Jack hadn't any better luck at the hotel. The two of them had waited all afternoon in the lobby the day the prince and Chelsey had run along the beach and later toured the city. So the two of them didn't see Chelsey. Michael hadn't returned to the hotel because when he'd visited Isadora at the palace—before the agents arrived—he'd found her in better spirits than he'd seen her for some time.

So he left the palace relieved, wondering only about the prince's reasons for bringing him and Chelsey to Beirut. He left the palace before José's men came and spent the rest of the day wandering through the city. By the time he'd returned to the hotel, José and Jack had given up and gone to dinner.

And after the crazy two-day game of phone tag, Michael had given up on trying to phone Jack. Besides, once he'd visited Isadora, he felt less reason to contact the newspaperman. No kidnapping had occurred, and Isadora was well. Plus, he was certain he and Chelsey would soon return to New York. She'd called him about the interview with Isadora. Although Chelsey's voice sounded a bit strange, distant, he wasn't concerned. Michael figured she was distracted by questions she'd planned to ask the model. And the tidbit of news made him more hopeful. Once Chelsey had completed the interview, a spicy exposé, he was sure, about the model's new-found happiness, he was sure the two of them would find a way out of this city. After all, since they'd surrendered and returned with Ishmael, the prince had been lax about restricting them. On the other hand, because El Fashid had taken off from work to spend his every waking hour with Chelsey, he needed to hire no one else to guard her. She wasn't left alone long enough to slip away, let alone talk much to Michael. At first, this bothered Michael, but later he saw her ploy. This distracted the prince so Michael could plan their escape. And he needed merely to plot the most foolproof plan, then slip in one night after the prince left Chelsey's room and explain it to her.

This morning, he lumbered along the beach and enjoyed the smell of the sea, the sun against his back, and the mist spraying his face. Even with the chaos of the last week, he felt more relaxed than he had in an incredibly long time. He'd decided that once he returned to the Apple he'd start taking off a little more time. No more working weekends and working till nine p.m. most nights. He'd rarely stayed away from work for a full weekend over the past few years. In fact, he'd been stockpiling leave every year as if it were a commodity. He'd accrued more than nine months of vacation. Oddly enough, when he'd phoned the office, not even the publication's owner was concerned he'd be gone awhile. Of course, he hadn't told him he'd been kidnapped. *No, that would've showed lack of control.* Instead, Michael had feigned an emergency arising overseas—his overseas accounts were muddled, he'd lied. "Take your time," Gregor, the owner had said. "We'll manage. You haven't taken time off in a year. In fact, I've been waiting for a call informing me you'd had a heart attack."

Michael took the hint. In fact, he decided taking time off was probably now his best career move. So he meandered around the beach, enjoyed the soft winds and watched the gulls soaring overhead. Then, he spotted an odd van cruising the road that ran down the hill. It was a light green Dodge Caravan. The color struck him—he'd seen none like it. Not only was it ugly, it stood out in this setting. He hadn't seen any other tourists in a vehicle like that, either. Then, it seemed as if the van slowed and started keeping pace with him. He wondered why. Perhaps the prince hadn't given them as much freedom as he'd assumed, he thought. He couldn't see the driver and wondered if it were Ishmael. *Or maybe the prince had hired another man to stalk him,* he considered.

Then, as the van came closer, he could see two men inside it. One of them looked like an American. So instead of trying to lose the vehicle, Michael started walking toward it. As he approached the van, he lifted a hand to shade his eyes, then he squinted and spotted Jack. Well, it looked like his old friend Jack, except his hair had grown white, and he'd added about fifty pounds.

Jack stared and appeared to recognize him. The van stopped, and Jack got out and waved both arms. "Michael!" he yelled, and Michael loped up to him.

"Well, fellah." Jack clapped him on the back. He shoved a shot glass toward Michael. "You don't look any worse for wear, if you can pardon the cliché and the pun." He laughed a deep, Jack laugh, one with snorts that sounded like a bulldog breathing.

"I've been trying to reach you at *The Globe*." Michael shook his head. "It's been insane trying to connect."

"Phone connections are lousy here. They need Ma Bell." Jack pulled out his pipe and lit it. "I thought you were abducted."

"I was." Michael grinned. "But Chelsey's occupying the prince so I can plan our getaway."

"He lets you wander around like this?" Jack wrinkled his brow and puffed on his pipe.

"He's no fool." Michael sighed. "He knows I won't leave without Chelsey. And he's with her every minute. In fact, I worry about her—

she may be falling for that sheik. She allows him to rub her back, hug her, and play with her dog."

"So how's she holding up?"

"She seems interested, but I believe she's onto his charm. How he manipulates women with it. So I think everything's okay. Don't get to talk to her much, though."

"What about Isadora?"

"Chelsey's interviewing her today. She wasn't kidnapped after all."

"I heard." Jack puffed on his pipe again.

"Should be a good story anyway: Model Finds Peace in the Middle East." Michael grinned. "Actually, she's doing better than I've ever seen her. She hasn't had a cigarette in weeks. And she quit drinking vodka. No more coke or downers, either."

José honked. Jack glanced back at the van. "Hey, c'mon with us. Let's get some food and talk." He nodded toward the vehicle. "That's the CIA agent I told you about. We'll get you guys out of this mess—today."

CHAPTER 33
Plunging toward Earth

Dardiel and Liwet sat behind the control panels of the huge ship now headed toward Jerusalem. It'd been centuries since the two had visited the city, and both eagerly scanned the starlit skies for it. Every now and then, a comet streaking across their screen distracted them, but soon they were back keeping watch for the silent planet. After what seemed like an eternity, at least to Liwet, they approached the northern half of the globe. Finally, as they grew closer, they saw Jerusalem's rooftops glimmering now in the twilight. Reflecting a spectrum of reds, yellows, lavender, and blues, the rooftops twinkled as if they were dancing. And in all its glory, the city spread across the hills. Tall pines, palms, olive and fig trees dappled the landscape of white and beige stone buildings with red tile roofs trickling down the slopes, running like tributaries toward a sea. They had approached the city from the north, so when they saw lights from their ship reflect off the golden dome on the Temple of the Rock, it helped their keen eyes spot Golgotha, where the Church of the Holy Sepulchre now stood. The stone wall separating the Old City from the new one wound around the city, looking somewhat like a huge ribbon looping around the outside box containing a huge, special gift—an entire world, actually--for a loved one. And the gift would come from a king at least. Not even a prince could provide it.

"Beautiful," remarked Liwet. "It's so romantic, too."

"Romantic?" Dardiel glanced at his colleague and sighed. "That would not have been my word choice. But I agree the city's beautiful." When they arrived at the spot directly above Golgotha, about ten miles above the earth, he shifted the controls into a hover mode, stood and stretched his wings. "Whew! Such a long ride. My wings have cramped a bit."

Liwet stood also and flickered his wings, then began pacing the cabin. "Should I check the arms again? I'll make sure all munitions are in place."

"Why?" Dardiel smiled. He'd discerned Liwet's true desires. "None of the *homo sapiens* will arrive here—not even the old ones— for another twelve hours."

"True. But I'm feeling antsy. We don't have much to do for a while." Liwet's voice squeaked higher than usual. "And it won't hurt to make sure everything's spiff."

"Then, go ahead if you must. The exercise will be good for you." Dardiel bent over and stretched again, swooping first his right arm and wing across his torso, then his left arm and wing the other way. He repeated the stretches seven times then lifted back up. "And Gabriel and the King will arrive early, I am certain," he added. Then he flew to the window and for a while, studied the scene on earth. "I will prepare the laser escalators for their descent to the crust of the planet."

Liwet strolled back toward the arms of the skycraft. Actually, he was fairly certain everything was prepared, but he wanted to check out their handiwork once more—the smooth steel walls, the mirrored glass with its etched trim. Never before had he helped to remodel such an enormous project. He struggled to control feelings of pride. Of course, he'd only been one of the workers. Still, when he scanned the mirrored glass walls with shimmery steel edged again, he marveled. Finished to perfection, the lab where the two had studied slides and dissected specimens and in fact, had spliced a variety of botanical species, sometimes rare orchid strains, other times, tomato and potato stalks to help mitigate famines on earth and other planets, now served as the hub of the space cruiser. *It is beautiful*, he thought.

Stretching five-hundred yards long, the ship contained two arms on either side, each fifty feet wide, that each extended two hundred feet from the main body. Each arm would serve as a sleeping area, one for the males, the other, for the females. The mirrored glass covered the sides from halfway down, and huge sections made up the bottom of the cruiser, too. But the synthetic steel girders bolstered it. Indeed, the structure could sustain several thousand tons of weight. The main section still contained computers and equipment for those who wanted to continue studies. There, most of the earthlings would mingle until they arrived on Serkerpia. An extensive library of books and DVDs that could be shown on the built-in video screens would help keep the travelers occupied. Dining tables and lounge chairs were arranged in patterns that would be conducive to socializing, too. At the very back, lay a locked room with thirteen chests, each shaped like a shofar, where valuables would be stored, just in case some passengers hadn't yet found the faith to realize no one coming into the ship would even think of stealing anyone's possessions.

He tromped through the right aisle, opened storage cabinet doors and doors to the linen closets, where he patted down and smoothed the comforters. He flew up to the ceiling, stopped at each berth, and checked to ensure a guide book was under each pillow. Sometimes, he'd pump up a pillow or two, especially if they looked a little flat, then carefully, he'd position each one back in place. *They must look inviting*, he thought. Probably, a number of the *homo sapiens* will be a bit nervous at first, and they may feel more comfortable hiding in here. Now and again, he'd stop at a window and linger a few minutes. He looked down at the globe below, study its changing colors, and watched the stars move like chariots across the heavens. He wondered when they'd start falling. He heard Dardiel call, "Liwet!" in his thin voice that echoed through the chambers and reverberated against the glass. "Bring me a pillow. I want to stretch out on the floor when I watch the show."

"Oh yes! Be there shortly!" replied Liwet, glad that Dardiel had reminded him. He'd become so involved in checking out the ship, he'd nearly forgotten this portion of the mission. Dardiel, Gabriel, Michael, and he were the most fortunate ones of his species. He felt so thankful when he remembered this treat. From all the others, for some reason, Emeth had chosen the four of them to enjoy the upcoming spectacle— the most lavish one the universe had presented in millenniums. It'd fill the sky with a thousand times more light than the largest meteor show. Huge explosions of fiery rain would sizzle across the heavens. Although the *homo sapiens* weren't yet aware of it, this huge fireworks display was about to start. And he, Dardiel, the other two Serkerpians, and the *homo sapien* passengers about to join them, would have the best—certainly the safest—seats in the house.

CHAPTER 34
True Love at Last

Chelsey was uncertain whether she should tell the prince about her visitor. Perhaps, she thought, it'd feed his delusion. Surely, it must be a delusion, a hallucination from all the stress his father and the distribution business put him under. She no longer considered him crazy because after all, if he were, so was she. And for the rest of the evening and the next day after Gabriel had appeared in her parlor, she'd analyzed the situation: Both of them hadn't slept enough lately. *That was it; surely it was. People could lose their minds from lack of sleep.* She'd read about it, and she'd once interviewed an expert on sleep deprivation, then used the info to help the police find a criminal who manipulated victims by depriving them of sleep. Sleep deprivation was indeed a weapon. People sometimes murdered others because they were sleep-deprived.

On the other hand, the prince had claimed he'd seen the beings a couple of months before, and the one—Gabriel as he called himself—again recently. Also, so far, no one else had mentioned the beings—neither the servants nor Ishmael, no one connected with this alien city. Such ideas battled each other in her head that night and all the next day, leaving her even more weary. She'd wanted to tell Michael about the event in her suite, but she didn't dare, especially now. Not after what happened two days later.

That morning, the prince had stopped by with fresh orchids to put in her vases. But instead of going out for breakfast, he'd phoned room service to save time because he had to take care of "business" in his office, he'd said. He asked if they could they meet two hours later at a gallery both of them especially liked. After he left, it dawned on her she needed to phone Michael—she'd not yet told Michael that the prince was allowing them to leave. Even though it was 7:30 a.m., the publisher picked up on the first ring.

"About time," he barked. "Don't you check messages? I've left them about every hour."

"I turned off my phone—no satellite tower here."

"What about your smart phone?"

"It won't work here."

"The phone in your suite?"

"You left messages here? The light hasn't blinked."

"It probably doesn't work. But—hey, I'm sure it recorded my message. You haven't checked your mailbox downstairs, either, I suppose."

"I'm sorry. I didn't know we had to ask." Chelsey sighed. "I'm surprised the clerk didn't say anything."

Michael continued his rant. "I've come by your suite several times, too. And I couldn't leave a message on the door because the wrong person might see it. Never mind that now. Guess who's in town?"

"Jack."

"You knew?"

"Yes," she mumbled, embarrassed now. "I saw him with you when you left the other day in that ugly van."

Michael shook his head. "I can't believe you haven't contacted us." He clipped his words. "What's going on anyway? Has he seduced you?"

"No—*no*—no!" Chelsey's chest tightened and her throat felt furry. She picked up a glass of water and swallowed a little of it. "He's been a true gentleman. It's just that since I talked with Isadora, I've needed time alone."

"You haven't been with the prince?" He raised his voice.

"Yes, most the time we're together. But not 24-7. Besides, why should that matter to you? It isn't as if I'm in danger. I'm safer with him than I am alone."

"Look—what's going on?" His voice boomed.

"Quit talking to me like that!" Her voice had grown louder now, too, surprising her more than it did Michael. "What right have you to make demands of me? You knew where I was—or in what vicinity most of the time. Besides, I'm not your protégé or anything. You act—you act as if you were my father!"

Michael exhaled so loudly, Chelsey heard his breath hit against the receiver. Then, in a softer tone, he added, "Why don't I come over before the prince returns, okay? Obviously, we need to talk. Today."

When Michael came in, his eyes looked bloodshot. At first, Chelsey thought he might have been drinking. But she smelled no alcohol, and then, she noticed his cheeks seemed to glisten a little, as if they were tear-stained. She reached out and squeezed one of his hands. "Are you all right?"

"Yeah. Let's sit down at the table, okay?"

After they sat a short while, Michael continued. "I should've told you this a long time ago—but I wasn't sure. And I didn't want to mess up your life, okay? I know I've been a cad, and I won't blame you for hating me—"

"You weren't very nice." Chelsey frowned. "Sure, I should've called you. But my life's upside-down now, okay?"

"I'm not talking about just now—although I worried when you didn't call. But something you said, well, it made me realize you need to know something."

Chelsey wrinkled her forehead. "I don't understand what you mean."

"I'm getting to it." Michael sighed. "I'm getting to it." He reached across the table and placed a palm on one of her forearms. "You know, I knew your mother before you were born."

"Yes. I knew. What does Mom have to do with this?"

"Everything. And I'm not even sure. She married Hank when she thought we'd never get back together."

"Yes. Neil told me that much."

"Good ol' Neil, yeah. She'd been better off marrying him, if not me." Michael sighed again. "Anyway, I didn't know your mother was pregnant. And I'm not quite sure because she and Hank got together so soon after we split up—but then, when I saw you in the prince's jet, well, you look like a combination of your mother—and of mine."

"What?"

"You get what I'm trying to say?"

Chelsey fell back against her seat. "Yeah," she said, then frowned again. "So all these years, you just avoided me—abandoned me, as if I were some stray you were trying to ditch. You let Neil raise me. And no wonder Hank never had much to do with me once Mom and I left." She shook her head, which started throbbing then. And she chewed on her lower lip to keep from crying. She didn't want to cry—not in front of him, not now. "I can't believe you—or anyone—would do such a thing!"

Tears filled his eyes, which grew more bloodshot, and his face reddened, too. "What can I say but 'I'm sorry. *Mea culpa.*' I can't do any more now. Like I said, Penny never told me for sure."

"Of course not." She'd started to cry now, too.

But Chelsey's tears were as much from anger as from sorrow. "She didn't want you coming to her for that. She wanted you to come because you loved her. Obviously, you didn't. And you didn't love your daughter, either."

"Hey—back off." Michael drew back his hand, put his elbows on the table, and leaned forward. "That isn't true. I loved you even when I didn't know for sure you were mine. But I had only a studio apartment in Brooklyn. It's no way to raise a kid."

"I wouldn't have minded. And I would've had a mother to raise me, too." Chelsey sobbed louder, now. She stood, sprang to the bed room, and closed the door. Michael heard her crying, but he didn't leave. After a while, he got up, shuffled to the bed room and lightly knocked on the door. "Again, I'm sorry. But hey—we've got to talk to Jack about getting a plane out of here. I'm ready any time."

"Then go." She sniffed but had quit crying.

"So where and when will you meet us?"

"I'm not."

"What?"

"I said, I'm not meeting you anywhere because I'm not leaving. Except with the prince—to Jerusalem." She crossed her arms.

"What?"

"That's why I couldn't talk with you." She went to the door, opened it, and looked up at him. Her hair was tousled, her eyes red, but her mouth was firm. "I couldn't decide what to do. I know now. I've decided. I'm staying."

"What's the big deal about Jerusalem?"

Chelsey smiled slightly. "You're Jewish and you're asking?" Then she smirked. "That's right, you don't practice."

He inhaled deeply. "It isn't too late, you know. We can start seeing each other now and—"

"Doubt I'll drop back into the Apple—ever."

"I could come to North Platte—"

"I won't be there, either." She shook her head, but looked at him and reached out and squeezed one of his hands. "Listen," she whispered. "I'm glad you told me. It helped me decide my future. I am joining the prince's heavenly journey."

CHAPTER 35
Ground Control

Michael, Jack, and José rode in the light green van that led the battalion of CIA agents in a caravan of BMWs to Golgotha in Jerusalem. Michael had talked to Isadora once more, and she'd readily revealed the meeting-place. Michael figured she wouldn't have told him that much had she known he was leading the CIA to the palace. Probably she'd thought Michael had merely asked out of curiosity. Or perhaps, she had hoped he'd join the space crew. *Probably not*, he reconsidered. In fact, she likely assumed he'd now catch a jet to the Apple and go home. He imagined she couldn't fathom that he'd be traveling there. He did not know yet about the space cruiser. But then, Isadora had known better than to mention the ship to Michael. She feared he would probably try to have her institutionalized again. She understood that he could never handle such other-worldly information, just as he couldn't deal with Chelsey staying with the prince.

This evening, though, he might have been open to that royal romance. Rapping his fingers on the back of Jack's seat, Michael felt ripped up, as if some loony with a buck knife were carving out his insides. The feeling wouldn't leave him as they rolled across the desert, then up and down the pine-covered hills. It fact, it remained within him when they came in from the north and approached the holy city's Damascus Gate.

Smoking his pipe, Jack sat in the suicide seat and mumbled over and over again, "I can't believe it. Such a talented reporter. Such a good kid. How could she? How could she do it? How could she throw away her career to go on some space shuttle to who knows where?" He shook his head repeatedly, as if he were one of those spring-necked toy dogs that bob on many travelers' dashes. Yet secretly, he wondered if she planned to write a story about the trip. He hoped she'd give *The Globe* an exclusive.

Neither José nor Michael answered him. Instead, they silently took in the view, with José checking his mirrors repeatedly to catch glimpses of the other five cars in the caravan. He worried whether he'd brought enough men to overtake any army the prince may have hired. *Probably, the playboy had started some cult and had hypnotized the two broads so they didn't want to leave him,* he thought, as he steered the van through the narrow streets. *Those spoiled, rich kids are all alike, whether Arab, Jew, or Gentile. Never having to work for a living or struggle to make ends meet or even to pick up a woman, they don't appreciate their privileges. They believe they can have whatever they want and bully everyone, even women and children.* But at last, the U.S. would set things right by defending its weaker vessels, and he would be a part of it. Whether it was such a thought or the adrenaline from the upcoming chase, he didn't know, but now, his chest swelled with pride, and he became more homesick for Arlington. So onward they drove, south-southwest, making their way through the city, this strange caravan of green cars, headed by the greenest, ugliest van local passersby had even seen.

Every now and then Michael glanced out the window at the night sky. Suddenly, out of nowhere, the largest, strangest shaped airplane— or some type of flying apparatus appeared several miles above the city. It was the largest plane he'd ever seen. But its edges weren't smooth like most jets. Its wings were long, rectangular boxes with blunt ends, like the early double-winged planes of more than a hundred years ago. In fact, it looked like a giant, shimmery silver cross that descended then hovered above the area where Michael was certain Golgotha was located. Most locals claimed it was buried under the Church of the Holy Sepulchre. "Look at that!" Michael said. "What it is? Some sort of UFO?"

"Aww, those things ain't real," José replied. "You've been smokin' too much pot." Nonetheless, he quickly looked through the windshield at the machine in the sky.

He blinked. Whatever it was, José had never seen anything like it. It looked like a plane from another age—except it was much larger, and it glowed so much.

"I'll be d——." Jack stopped mid-sentence and gaped as he looked at the sky. "Whatever it is, it's huge. It's so iridescent, wonder if it's made of platinum or titanium."

"Can we go any faster?" Michael asked. Since he'd spotted the flying machine, he hadn't looked away from it. He wondered why it seemed to hover over their destination, or whether it merely appeared to be near it. They were still too far away to tell. But the flying contraption shot out intense lights, more than any plane he'd seen; more than any rocket, either. "Perhaps it's some publicity act," he said, but his voice trailed off, as if even he didn't believe that explanation. Then, a terrifying thought struck him. He wondered if the prince was somehow behind the sky-ship's construction.

The parade of vans wound through the narrow streets, onward to their destination. Of course, none of the agents had anticipated meeting with any aerial contraption. They'd only expected to encounter an Arab army—perhaps terrorists, and they'd armed themselves with bullet-proof vests and Uzis for that. Each of them gawked when they peered out of the car windows, remarking how large the plane—or whatever— was and how intensely it shined. Some marveled it might be built of platinum—or some material not found on earth. Others speculated it might be a weapon the prince had paid terrorists to build, and they wondered why they hadn't caught wind of it from their Saudi Arabian agents.

When the men arrived at the spot, they saw hundreds of cars with people getting out of them to watch the object in the sky. The agents swung their vehicles into a circle and parked. But everyone continued watching the object in the sky. Some suggested it might shoot lasers out to incinerate them and wondered what they could do to stop it.

As soon as their van stopped, Michael, Jack and José disembarked. Like the others, they kept staring at the flying machine. It was a spectacular sight: It glowed and glimmered in various colors, shimmering like sapphires, rubies, and emeralds. The light it emanated became more and more intense as it descended, forcing the men to shield their eyes with their hands. Awe-struck, none of the agents moved very much. They merely stood there, their car doors left ajar, watching the cruise ship descending closer and closer.

Then, from across the way, Michael spotted the prince's limo. With Fatima sitting in the front passenger's seat, Ishmael swerved the long car into the lot. In the back, like everyone else, Chelsey, the prince, and Isadora watched the sky. They focused only on it and didn't see Michael, Jack and José.

"Hey guys—there they are!" Michael barked. He started moving toward the limo. José, Jack and the other men followed. But before they walked twenty feet, they stopped. The huge, sky object descended further, spinning up a gale that nearly knocked them over. It stopped and hovered about a mile above the earth, then sprayed streams of intense light brighter than laser beams, only they weren't straight beams but wobbled in all directions. In fact, the beams of light were shaped like a chain of human bodies in long robes linked together hand-in-hand, much like a child's cut-out of paper dolls. This laser chain of bodies flew up and into the ship. Then, after a while, when the flow of the human chain into the ship ceased, the strange air ship started descending again. It stopped again, this time about a half-mile from the earth. And from that strange ship, huge beams of intense, white light fell in every direction, dropping till the shafts of light hit the earth. Michael squinted and discerned that the ship wasn't merely shooting out rays of light. No, it was lowering some intensely bright escalators, which shimmered to form what looked like the outline of a Babylonian ziggurat. To the CIA men and Jack, it looked akin to a giant, whirling carousel, shooting out brilliant multi-colored beams to the earth. All of them stood, transfixed. Try as they might, not one of them could take even one step toward the ship.

CHAPTER 36
Ishmael and Fatima Repent

<u>Jerusalem, Israel: August 21, 2015</u>

After Chelsey had slid into the limo's back seat, Abdul clutched one of her hands and held it between both of his all the way to Jerusalem. Although the ride had been peaceful, the mood had been sad. Still, Jerusalem's ancient stone buildings and gates amazed Chelsey, who chided herself for not seeing this city before now. The olive and fig trees seemed bushier, lusher than those in Beirut, and the ancient temples and churches evoked peaceful feelings in her, even though the feelings were tinged with sorrow. The prince still had misgivings about whether the women would be safe, even after Chelsey had assured him that all would go well. The Goddess's faith had renewed Chelsey's strength and belief in herself.

Chelsey had also regained her confidence in being part of a plan beyond her tiny little world. She no longer feared her destiny. In contrast, the prince's sorrow went deeper than hers for it was mixed with guilt and anguish. Days before, he'd realized how much he didn't want her to go onto the ship. He wanted her to remain with him and become his princess. He'd miss her, he said, he didn't know how he could bear life without her, now, and he squeezed her hand harder.

"Why don't you come, too?" she asked and squeezed one of his hands, too, ran her fingers across its palms. She realized now she hadn't been as close to anyone in a long, long time. She'd miss him, too, immensely. And she might need his help on the trip.

"I can't." He hung his head. "They won't have me. Only those on the list may enter the ship."

"Have you asked?"

He shook his head and frowned. "No. They would have told me if my name were on the list." He knew he'd only been hired as a middleman. Once they paid him, he'd be sent away.

"Why not try anyway?" She frowned and stared at him.

He shrugged and looked into her eyes. "Yes, perhaps I can."

Chelsey turned away from him and looked out the window and gazed up at the sky. Although a pale white moon had risen, the sun still shined, but it soon grew red, then darkened with the rest of the sky. And instead of glowing brighter, the moon darkened, too, and it seemed the stars began falling. Then, at first, she thought she saw a huge thunderhead of clouds moving in. Then, after she studied the thunderhead, she could see it change into a glimmering spaceship shaped like a cross. She blinked. Indeed, the sky-craft was shaped not quite like a regular jet, but like a giant cross with thick, wide wings like the early World War I fighters. Yet this ship was much, much larger. Finally, she saw the shimmering, human chains that looked like lasers flowing into the ship.

"Look!" she said and Scout barked, in a lower tone, sounding almost like a trumpet. "They've come. Isn't it fantastic? I wonder what metal that ship contains. It's so iridescent, almost like an opal."

The prince drew his hand away and pressed his fingers together as if in prayer. He intermittently looked at the ship and then at Chelsey.

Awed by the intense light, Ishmael gazed up, and Chelsey saw tears in his eyes. His mouth gaped, and then, mumbled something, like a chant, over and over, but Chelsey couldn't understand his words. Simultaneously, Fatima dug furiously in her purse and pulled out what looked like a long, beaded necklace, then she nodded her head and clutched what Chelsey could see was a rosary between her red fingernails. She pressed her hands, interwoven now with the rosary, against her breasts. She cried, too, bowed her head and Chelsey thought she heard the woman pray, "Oh my Lord, forgive my sins." Tears ran down her cheeks as she continued between sobs, "Forgive me for my wretched, horrible life."

Ishmael watched her without speaking. Then he turned and watched the descending sky ship. For a long while, he said nothing. But his dark eyes opened wider, and Chelsey saw his face fill with terror. Finally, he wailed, "Ai-ee!" And suddenly, the large man shoved open a door and slipped outside the limo, where he dropped to his knees. He bowed low to the ground till he lay prostrate. He prayed in Arabic and continued lifting his torso then bowing, back and forth, moving to the rhythm of his prayers.

Chelsey watched Ishmael pray while her gaze simultaneously followed the cruise ship's descent to the ground. Before it landed, it appeared to shoot out rays that looked like lasers. Then, she saw that the rays were actually escalators that glowed so intensely, they merely appeared to be rays of light. She looked across the way and became amazed at what she saw there, too. Michael, Jack, and another man stood beside the ugly green van, which a circle of cars had surrounded. She wondered why they had come here and if Michael hadn't believed her when she said she wouldn't return to the states. Perhaps he thought the prince had hypnotized her and still held her captive. She smiled now at the thought. She'd let him know that she was okay when she disembarked.

"It's time," she said and turned to the others. Ishmael sprang up, scurried to the back of the can, opened the trunk, and then came around to the side. He picked up Isadora and her bags, then gently set them on the ground. While the group stood beside the trunk, staring at the marvelous machine above, Michael rushed toward them.

"Wait!" he yelled. He sounded out-of-breath as he neared the limo.

He ran to Chelsey and wrapped his arms around her. "You don't have to leave." He shook his head. "Are you sure you want to do this?"

She nodded. "Why don't you come, too? You're on the list. That's why they took both of us. You, the Goddess, and I are all on the passenger roster."

Michael stared at her a minute, then glanced at Jack and José, who waited with his pistol in hand. After a while, he looked back at Chelsey and finally, at Isadora. The Goddess smiled. She glowed. "I-I-I," he stuttered. "I dunno." Then, he looked back at Jack once more and waved. "Go on," he yelled. "It's all right. We're fine here. We don't need anyone's help. No one is being abducted. We're all leaving on the ship of our own accord. Everything is okay!"

José and Jack stared at each other, then looked around at the other men. They stared at the ship with mouths gaped.

Jack shook his head. "I don't get it. Now, he's flipped out, too. What's happening to all these people. And why did my legs lock when I tried to walk toward that crazy airplane? Something weird is going on here." Nonetheless, no one appeared to be coercing Michael—or Chelsey—to board the strange machine. Jack sighed. Then he grinned. "I'll bet they just want to get a good story." He shrugged and looked at José. "They'll be back, then. And if they're clever and we're lucky, we'll all learn something from this crazy event."

"Okay guys! False alarm!" José yelled. "We can go now. We can go back to the office. And some of you can go home." None of the agents moved. They may have figured, they'd come this far, they might as well watch the action. Besides, the feds would have to work out a story to tell the public about this giant UFO. It was their duty to the public. Many of them spoke at once about ideas concerning the ploy. Maybe we could say the Russians built it, one of them suggested. But another thought it'd be better to blame it on the Israelis. One other man thought the Chinese should shoulder the blame.

The others moved toward the ship and stepped upon one of the laser escalators. When they approached the cabin, Gabriel welcomed them by fluttering his wings, but he asked the prince to step aside. When a lull occurred, Gabriel turned to him. Discretely, he gave Abdul the promised money, rolled up neatly and tied with a scarlet ribbon. The prince crammed it into his pocket, then looked back at Chelsey. She stood holding Scout, pulling one of his paws up and down to wave goodbye to Jack. The prince frowned, kissed Chelsey's cheek, then dashed out of the ship, and rode an escalator back to the ground.

CHAPTER 37
Take-off

Up in the sky cruiser's cabin, Liwet fidgeted. He watched the *homo sapiens* filling the escalators. He spotted Chelsey, the prince, and the Goddess. "What if those men chasing Chelsey and the prince try to hop aboard?"

"They will not." Dardiel replied and crossed his arms. "They could not do so if they tried, not even if they used all the ammunition on the earth.

"What will stop them?" Liwet wings flickered wildly with his agitation.

"Their fear. They were not called because they refused to listen to the small, still voice inside each of them. They were not chosen because they set their minds on earthly visions. They do not know *love*, so they fear us. That fear will reign them in."

Liwet still stared at the scene below. His eye sockets pinched at their tops to become tight, elongated triangles. They raised most of the laser elevators now, just three more of them touched the ground while the last of the passengers loaded.

Back in the passengers' area, Scout licked Chelsey's hands and he stretched toward one of her cheeks. She patted his nose but wouldn't let him lick her face. She smiled. "It's okay, Boy. Everything's fine, now." She positioned the dog on a shoulder so he could look back at the earth. She hoped the prince was okay. She'd miss him, yes. But the rest of the life back there, she wasn't so sure. This would certainly be a new life—frightening in one way. But she had a purpose—one that would impact millions of people. And ironically, in lieu of feeling burdened, she felt the greatest sense of freedom and peace she'd felt in her short life on earth. Still positioning Scout so he could see out the huge window, she turned to scan the crowd. More people that she would've imagined milled around the huge lobby.

"Hello," an older man said to her. She blinked. It was Neil.

"You're here?"

"Yeah." He grinned the silly grin that made him appear to be all teeth. "Guess I was called." Then, he shook his head. "But I can't imagine why."

They hugged and for a while, Neil held the dog, while through the lower mirrored panes, Chelsey watched what was happening below.

***

On the ground, the prince was miserable. He glanced around at the spectators who watched the ship, but made no moves toward it. One man in a pin-striped, Armani suit lifted his chin in the air. "Those people are idiots," he said, his voice booming, "not knowing just where they're going. It's safer here, even if it's not perfect." His pin-striped colleague nodded. Clutching a briefcase, the latter glanced at his watch and looked back at the ship still hovering a few feet above the ground. The prince moved away from them—Chelsey thought he probably could no longer stand their thick, acrid smells. She watched his eyes fill with tears as he stared at the ship and where Chelsey sat. He looked down at his hand and the roll of bills he still clutched. His father would be proud, Abdul was sure, but he hated himself and wanted to throw this blood money to the wind. Instead, he looked back at the ship and the escalator rays. Then, without thinking further, he ran toward the only last ray still near the ground. The last of the passengers still rode it, and it had begun to lift and pull back into the cruiser. He ran faster, but stumbled over an olive tree branch, catching a sliver of the bark in his palm. He steadied himself, stood and sprinted onward.

He ran and ran, panting now, gasping for breath, and then, as he approached the ray, he leapt with all the strength he could muster. His arms were outstretched, but still clutched the rolls of bills. He flew higher than he'd anticipated, then landed face-down upon the escalator ray. At first, he felt his knees and elbows burn, as if he'd scraped them on concrete. But the warm laser heat soothed them and soon, he was able to crawl to his knees, then finally, stand. He felt a terrible fool now and was sure the throngs below laughed at him. He didn't care. He'd learned to accept humiliation. But then, he started worrying the beings wouldn't let him in the ship. If so, this final burst of effort was worthless. But if he did not try, he would regret it for the rest of his life.

Gabriel stood at the entrance again. The prince pushed the roll of bills into one of the Serkerpian's hands. "Take it," he said. "Or could I use it as my fare?"

"We don't allow fares here," Gabriel said, "only those who are called may come. *Only those who are chosen.* Money has no play in this." He handed the roll back to the prince.

Tears filled Abdul's eyes. First, he looked back at Chelsey and stared a few minutes. He looked down at the roll, fingered the money, and handed it back to Gabriel. "I don't want it anyway. It is only paper. And if it were a Krugerrand or a thousand of them, I would not take the pay."

Gabriel laughed so loudly the door frame shook. "Very good!" He wrapped an arm around the prince and guided him toward the foyer, where Chelsey sat. "You are most welcome here, my friend. Especially, now." He slipped the roll back into the prince's pocket. "Enjoy the ride—and your new life."

Abdul ran to Chelsey, and both of them now teary-eyed, they embraced, squeezing Scout between them. Then, they took a seat beside one of the windows and together looked through it to watch the cruise ship rise steadily from the earth.

"Look," the prince pointed at the earth.

Chelsey looked back at the globe that had been her home for more than twenty years. She noticed red and yellow flames popping up on it. Then, they exploded like sun spots. *What was happening there?* she wondered and pointed it out to Abdul.

"It is happening as it was written," he said. The prince patted Scout on the head, then squeezed Chelsey's arm gently. Together, they watched the planet grow smaller and smaller, till nothing was left but a fiery ball, gleaming as if it were a falling star.

Chelsey smiled, leaned back in her seat and opened Erica's bible. She read *Luke* 10:2: "The harvest truly is great, but the laborers are few: pray ye therefore the Lord of the harvest, that he would send forth laborers into his harvest." And she wondered if they were to being shipped to become laborers somewhere—and for whom?

CHAPTER 38
Oops!

Had Chelsey heard Jack's remark when he watched Chelsey and Michael enter the ship, she would have been impressed to learn how well he knew her. She wasn't sure about Michael's motives, but she'd hopped this space cruiser for the story. She'd told neither Jack nor Michael—and certainly not Prince Abdul—that she hadn't believed in its "heavenly" destination. She'd sensed this gig was a fake—a "vain imitation" of the harvest forecast in *Revelation*. It wasn't real, she was sure, and she was taking this trip to unravel the back-story. She also wondered about the "other-worldly" beings, who now acted as the cruisers' stewards—or stewardesses, their genders being imperceptible. *What were they? Where did they come from? And what mastermind created this strange airship?* If the passengers were going to be sold into slavery, she must find a way to prevent it. For that, she'd need help, including from Prince Abdul. So she was especially glad he joined her. She knew Michael and Neil could help her overthrow whatever tyrant had staged this venture. First, though, she had to put together pieces before she could work with the others to abort the mastermind's Draconian plan.

Jack had trained her to "follow the money" and she adhered to that adage when she investigated nearly all stories. It had become a mode of thinking for her when she perceived most events, too, especially when she analyzed popular trends. She noticed how all the fanfare and ballyhoo over "gluten" and "gluten-free" products occurred during wheat crop failures. *Didn't the farming industry need less demand for wheat then?* And corn. She didn't understand why it was added to everything, including coatings for fresh fruits and vegetables merely to make them "lock fresher," except perhaps so farmers would be able to maintain selling prices for crops. And the sugar industry was behind cyclamates being removed from the market. Ironically, cyclamates were safer than aspartame. But the sugar corporations owned that sweetener. *And the oil industry—ha!* Even back in John D. Rockefeller's day, companies and commodities investors contrived plans not based on availability or supply-demand to raise oil prices, which had plummeted once everyone started drilling oil. DeBeers did the same in the diamond mines, with $2 billion stockpiles of diamonds in the 1980s. *Who knows what they were now?* she thought.

Likewise, she knew someone was behind today's joyride on this expensive airship, designed to imitate the true harvest that certainly wasn't yet on the horizon. Once more, many believers were being duped, just as they were by Jim Jones and other cult leaders. But here, she couldn't figure out why—and who would gain anything from this operation. She closely observed the beings who served them.

"My name is Liwet," said the one standing near her seat. "May I bring you a beverage or a dinner?"

"You're offering us *real* food?" Chelsey smiled. "This is like flying when I was a little girl in the early nineties."

Liwet nodded. "Oh yes. This flight will be as close to perfect as possible. Our menu offers an array of choices for your dinner."

After Abdul and Chelsey ordered prime rib, Chelsey smiled broadly, then squinted at the being for a long time. She detected a hairline scratch on his neck near where a human ear would be. But it wasn't like scratch on the skin of a human or another mammal. No, it looked as if the surface of a latex sculpture were scratched. She'd seen damage like that on one of the moving statues of Apollo, Venus, and Bacchus at Caesar's Palace, back in the late nineties.

Although she hadn't been old enough to gamble, Neil had taken her there to join him in sightseeing when he took time away from a convention he'd organized for one of the news associations. And when the casino changed to new statues, some of the older ones were left in a display in a forum. She examined the old statues closely and discovered why they were being replaced. Cracks rimmed the necks of the old statues. And those statues at Caesar's were made of the same material as these beings: latex, hard latex.

Obviously, then, these creatures weren't "beings" at all. They were machines—robots. And someone had created the Avatars who manned this ship. That person was indeed a genius to create beings who moved in such a lifelike manner. With their quick and natural responses, they appeared to be so natural—except for their eerie, squeaky voices. Now, those voices sounded mechanical, like a tape played at too high a speed. She wondered how the beings appeared to think when they responded to human words. Had their creator—or creators—installed electronic brains, somewhat like vehicle brains, but far more sophisticated? Were they all connected to a network? Where was it located? She chuckled quietly when she thought of Orwell's "Group Speak." These beings were part of a Group Think.

She also wondered about the being called "Gabriel," likely after the archangel. The one who "appeared" in her hotel room couldn't have been fashioned from latex: It was too translucent. But perhaps her early impulse was right. When he "appeared," he well might have been a hologram. It was likely a latex version that greeted them at the entrance today. That version of Gabriel seemed as solid as the other beings running the airship.

But who would have contacted the hotel and set up that hologram? And where were they being taken? She didn't believe the destination was anywhere other than somewhere on earth. Surely, the pilot was following a flight plan. Or perhaps the plane was remotely controlled.

After finishing dinner, which Chelsey admitted was as close to perfect as any prime rib she'd eaten, she called Liwet back to her seat. "You were right." She smiled coyly. "This is perfect."

Liwet nodded. "We do our best to please the Chosen Ones."

"Really?" Chelsey lifted her eyebrows. "There is something I would like very much to do on this ship. But I am not sure that is possible."

"What would that be?"

"Does the pilot allow you to give us tours?" She smiled and stared into his face. It looked as if onyx stones formed his eyes—or the encasements for "eyes." They looked real. *And at least, the controller had programmed the beings to be friendly, obsequious, even*, she thought then continued, "Or at least, to explore the plane? This ship is so huge, I'd like to see all of it—to explore all the different rooms. And, if it wouldn't disturb the captain, I'd like to see the cockpit."

Liwet looked at her a long time. He didn't blink or show any expression. Finally, he responded. "I will check with our captain, My Lady. And if he allows the tour, I would be most honored to guide you through the ship myself." He bowed again and waddled down the aisle, waiting on other passengers along the way.

Abdul looked at her. "You have become very interested in our future." He smiled and lifted a hand to Chelsey's cheek. "I am so glad I joined you. You are a wise woman. I would have never asked had you not encouraged me. I was sure I was not a godly-enough person to be admitted to this journey. Your faith in me gave me more faith."

Chelsey ached to tell him that she believed being gullible and passive had far more to do with gaining entrance to this flight. But she chewed on her lower lip and said nothing. Then she smiled and placed one of her hands over his. "You are a kind person. And quite generous."

His face brightened. "Thank you. I am most honored to hear those words from you. I understand that you do not throw away compliments like napkins in the wind."

Chelsey smiled again at the allusion.

"Would you like me to accompany you on the tour of the ship?"

" Well, uh . . ." Chelsey bit her lip again. "I'd love to have you join me. But I think it might be best if you rested now." she placed a hand on his knee. "We will spend so much time together later. And if you wouldn't mind, it may be best if you kept Scout here. He might create a ruckus in the cockpit."

"Ah, yes." The prince smiled again. "Our little friend. Yes, he will likely become bored on the tour and let his curiosity get him into trouble. I will be happy to perform this service for you."

Chelsey smiled once again when Liwet appeared again to give her a tour.

CHAPTER 39
Serkerpia: Home of the Brave

Chelsey was surprised she'd encountered so little resistance to her request to tour the space cruiser. On the other hand, if her request had been denied, she might have created an uproar. Such a scene might cause many passengers, especially her friends, to question the ship's destination. Most likely, the mastermind had considered that and found it easier to give his permission. She wondered why some of her friends came on this trip. Seeing Neil board the ship especially perplexed her. He'd always been a skeptic. Perhaps he'd joined the crew as a scientific experiment, or perhaps he'd appeared because he worried about her. When she could break away from the prince, she'd talk to Neil about his decision to come along.

In the cockpit, she found no sky map, no flight plans posted on the walls or anywhere prominent. However, she noted that both the pilot and co-pilot needed no breaks. They imbibed neither coffee nor food. No remnants of food lie near their chairs or control panels. She'd never seen a pilot fly without coffee. Even more revealing was a small outlet near the seat. When she first stepped into the room, the co-pilot quickly unplugged an adaptor that connected to something on his body. It wasn't an I-pod or phone, she was sure. She'd have to look at these beings more closely, she decided, to see if their bodies had plugs for re-charging them. If so, this situation would help her devise a *coupe*.

She smiled at the captain and co-pilot. "It's amazing that the two of you can maneuver such a huge ship. I couldn't imagine handling something so powerful."

"We are but part of a greater power." The captain nodded. "Without Him, we could do nothing."

That has more than just a figurative meaning for you, I bet, Chelsey thought but said nothing. She smiled again.

"The flight has already been programmed into the airship," the co-pilot said. "It works much like a GPS on one of your automobiles."

Chelsey nodded. "I understand." She slid between the two chairs holding the pilots and placed a hand on each one. "I wonder how fast this ship goes."

Neither the captain nor the co-pilot responded. They stared ahead.

She looked at the instrument panel but found nothing that looked like a speedometer. Other digital meters blinked red and green numbers, apparently indicating the cabin's air pressure and oxygen level, and probably the fluid levels on all the engines. She wasn't sure how to read any of the meters. Then she lowered her head between the seats so that it was level with theirs. "How long will our flight take?"

The co-pilot and captain looked at each other. It became obvious to

Chelsey that neither had anticipated a passenger would bring up this question. Or perhaps the pilots were not programmed to reply to it. Finally, the captain said, "Do you mean in light years or in earthly time?"

"Earthly time will be fine." She smiled again.

"It will require approximately 26 hours—earthly hours."

Chelsey nodded and scanned the instrument panel again. If she could find the speed, she could figure how far this ship was going. Perhaps Abdul could help her calculate its speed. He'd flown enough that he might be able to determine that by the feel of the ship. It was more important that she talk with Michael and Neil. Neither of them would be disappointed to learn what she'd discovered. And she knew it would likely break the prince's heart.

***

She was able to locate Michael first. She pulled him into a corner near one of the restrooms. "I've figured out what's going on."

"Really?" He smiled. "I thought you were ready for the Pearly Gates." He scratched his head and leaned in toward her. "What have you discovered?"

"I still don't know what's planned for the passengers—likely we'll be made slaves," she whispered. "But those beings are latex. I believe they're robots—or Avatars controlled remotely by someone. But I still haven't gleaned who he is—or where the controller is located. Or if there's a group of controllers. Or its true destination. I wonder if it's somewhere on earth."

"Anything else?"

"We'll land in a day—another 24 hours."

"I've done some research, too."

"Really? What?"

"I went online and found who invested in this ship. It's a firm in China—but don't laugh."

"Why?"

"It's northwest of Chungking." Michael grinned. "Really. On the edge of the mountain range."

"So there's no heavenly trip?" Chelsey smiled.

"I didn't figure you believed that. Did you?"

"No. But seeing Gabriel in my hotel room shook me for awhile."

"When did this happen?"

"A few days ago. That's when I realized the prince wasn't lying. Someone set up a hologram of Gabriel for him, too. That's why he believes this is for real. In fact, he feared he wouldn't be deemed 'worthy' to be a passenger."

"*Revelation*, huh?" Michael shook his head.

"Yes. But whoever is running this ship must be planning to enslave all of us."

"You mean more than our jobs do?" Michael grinned again then cleared his throat. "So how are we going to stop them?"

Chelsey explained how she believed the beings received their power. But she'd have to talk with Neil, and they'd have to break the news to the prince. Once they unplugged the beings, they'd need Abdul to fly the airship. "But one thing worries me," she added. "I'm not sure how we can dismantle the automatic controls. It could be that he won't be able to override them once we've dismantled the robots."

***

Even if Chelsey and Michael were careful to whisper out of range of Liwet, Dardiel, and the other iridescent beings, they had not paid enough attention to others who might eavesdrop upon their conversation. On the other side of the wall in the corner where they spoke, a human being posing as a passenger overhead every word they shared. His name was Albert Schwatzman, and he was the CEO of one of the investment corporations involved in the Heavenly Venture, the name the group of companies had given this endeavor. He had too much invested for it to fail.

So about two hours later, when Chelsey went back to the women's sleeping quarters, she stepped into a restroom and felt a thud on the back of her head. She collapsed, and a man in black stuffed Chelsey into a large garbage bag. The black-clad man also stretched a strip of duct tape across her mouth, injected Phenobarbital under her arm, and drug her into one of the airship's storage areas, which only the crew could access.

Capturing Michael was not as easy for Schwatzman. He waited until Michael dozed off then slipped into a seat behind him. While the other passengers slept, he drugged Michael in the same way. But moving Michael would prove more difficult. Thus, he stopped Liwet when the being performed his routine check.

"Liwet, this man here is ill." Pressing a hand upon Michael's shoulder, the black-clad man feigned concern. "As you can see, he's lost consciousness. We must transport him to the infirmary. I will keep watch over him there."

Dutiful Liwet brought a gurney and three other beings to carry Michael to the medical station. There the man stayed by Michael's side, ready to re-inject him whenever he regained consciousness. So neither Michael nor Chelsey were awake when the airship landed in Serkerpia. It was a gentle landing, but some of the passengers were not ready to disembark. The prince, for one, was frantic. He'd searched for Chelsey from the moment he awoke. But no one had seen her.

Stopping to sniff here and there, Scout scampered around the ship. He followed Chelsey's scent to the storage room. There, he yapped until Prince Abdul ran up and restrained him. But Scout didn't want to leave. As the prince picked up the dog, he heard rustling behind the door and insisted that it be opened. Liwet and two other beings ran to him and quickly threw open the door. Inside, a black plastic bag wriggled and bounced. Liwet untied it, and a sweaty Chelsey shook her head. The prince gently unpeeled the tape from her mouth.

"My head hurts," she whined. "I don't know what happened, but when I started toward the bathroom, something hit me. Just now, I just woke inside this stupid bag. I could barely breathe. What is going on?"

Liwet and the other beings huddled around her. One of them brought a cold cloth and pressed it on Chelsey's forehead.

The prince rubbed her hands and cooed soothing words. He no longer believed the trip was a heavenly mission. *Something was wrong here,* he realized. They'd been duped—all of them. And he was ready to fight to defend his beloved's life.

***

While the other passengers grabbed bags and prepared to disembark, the prince and Chelsey looked around for Michael. Chelsey found Neil, who helped search for the editor. But first, he tugged Chelsey toward one of the windows and nodded at the landscape outside the plane. A mountain range edged the green-cover hills and rolling landscape beyond the airport terminal. In the distance about fifteen miles, what looked like a city of gold gleamed in the evening sun. Edged by the green hills, it was a beautiful city containing several huge, red eight-sided pagodas stretching to the skies. It looked magical, but Chelsey worried about what that lovely city was likely hiding and where they would soon be. *In some factory chained to a wall?*

"Welcome to Serkerpia," the intercom said. "The stewards will escort you to your ground transportation that will lead you to your new homes. Please exit slowly—and only with a steward accompanying you."

Chelsey and Neil returned to the prince. "We cannot leave without Michael. Something's wrong here."

When Liwet heard the name "Michael," he rushed to the small group. "Do you mean Michael Levine, the man who you talked with yesterday?"

Chelsey nodded.

"He is not lost. He is in the medical station. Last night, he became ill and a man in black escorted him there."

"Will you take us to him?" Chelsey asked, her eyes wild.

"Of course." Liwet nodded and led the group back to the infirmary. There, Michael still slept.

"Are you okay?" Chelsey rushed to him and shook his shoulders. "What happened?"

Michael shook his head and blinked his eyes. "I-I-I . . ." He drew himself halfway into a sitting position and stared at each one of them. "What happened?"

Chelsey rubbed his shoulders and sighed. After a while, she spoke.

"Liwet, this steward here, said you became ill and someone brought you here." She tapped his back.

"Ill? I don't remember that. I fell asleep in my chair and had strange dreams. But I don't recall being nauseous or anything."

"The gentleman in black sitting behind you said you fainted," Liwet explained. "He came back with you. But I do not see him now." Liwet looked around the room. "He must have left the area."

Michael and Chelsey stared at each other. But they said nothing.

Once the foursome left the airship, Chelsey took Neil aside and asked why he'd agreed to take this journey.

"To keep an eye on you, of course." He grinned, revealing the buck teeth that Chelsey had grown up watching. They calmed her now.

She shivered. "How did you know I'd be here?"

"That information came with the invitation for me to join the cruise." He started to pull a paper from his pocket. "Would you like to see it?"

"Yes, definitely. Later." Then Chelsey explained what she and Michael had gleaned about the excursion. She looked around the cruiser cabin, then crossed her arms. "And not long after Michael and I talked, someone conked me on the head. We were careful not to let those beings hear us. I didn't see anyone near me, either. It wasn't one of the beings. All of them shine so brightly, I would have seen it light the room."

"I wonder who did it." Neil glanced around at the other passengers who now strolled toward limousines arranged in a long line at the edge of the airport. "There's enough of us to abort this mission—as long as we do it before we land, where armed guards will stop us."

"I wonder if some of the passengers aren't 'guests.' Who else could have hit me—and likely drugged Michael?" Chelsey scanned the crowd, too. "Someone must have overheard us. And that person didn't want us stopping this adventure."

Chelsey pulled out her android and clicked into the Internet. "Hey, I bet I can get a connection here." She looked at Neil and smiled. "It just dawned on me why this mastermind would want some of us."

Neil shrugged. "Why?"

Besides for slavery, why else do criminals kidnap humans?"

"A ransom?"

"This is bigger than that." She searched under "human trafficking" and "body parts." "Think about it, Isadora has a perfect body. Michael has incredible hearing and my eyesight is far above normal. Anyone with access to our medical charts could have discovered that."

Neil blinked and grinned.

Soon the prince caught up to them. "Are you okay?" he asked and wrapped an arm around Chelsey.

"Yes." She sighed. "We need to talk."

CHAPTER 40
The Prince Makes His Move

It was warm outdoors but not too hot. Although the temperature reached the low eighties, the humidity stayed low. Winds swooped down the mountains and drifted through the valley to make the air feel crisp. Had they not been in such a precarious situation, Chelsey would have loved being there. She told the prince about the feigned heavenly journey and hoped it wouldn't break his heart. She pulled him away from the crowd of persons moving like lemmings toward the golden city. She didn't want anyone to hear. Her head still ached from her last indiscretion.

Prince Abdul el Fashid was not crestfallen. "I have realized that, and I am so sorry. I should have known no angel has such a squeaky voice." Then, his face brightened and he squeezed one of her hands. "This means we could now marry and raise a family, correct?" he wrapped an arm around her shoulders.

Chelsey chewed on her lower lip. "Perhaps."

The prince smiled.

"First we must stop this abduction—or no one will marry." She glanced around and scanned the legion of bodies trudging on and on.

Most of them eyed the tall buildings, but some focused on the trail ahead. She saw Michael and Neil. They spotted her, too, and headed toward the prince and Chelsey. "We'll all be working in factories—or coal mines—or worse."

"No!" The prince crossed his arms. "We will not allow that."

She sighed and glanced around once again. "Listen, if we can somehow disable the beings and lure everyone back into the air-ship, would you be able to fly it?"

"Probably. But I am not absolutely certain." He shrugged. "First, I must see the control panels and study the monitors."

Although he didn't appear to be within hearing range, Albert Schwatzman still monitored Chelsey. First, he watched her from about thirty feet away and then slowly edged toward her. Chelsey noticed the man, whose bushy, white streaked hair and light blue eyes seemed vaguely familiar. She'd seen his face in the media, but she couldn't remember exactly where—or why. Still, she smiled broadly when she caught him eying her. Then she waved. "Come join us," she shouted.

Schwatzman stared at her, blinked, then turned and backed away from her. He smoothed his collar and acted as if he'd not been looking at Chelsey.

Immediately Michael was at her side. "Do you know who he is?"

"He's familiar—but I can't place him. It's been too long."

"Al Schwatzman, the world's richest entrepreneur. CEO of—"

"That's it," she interrupted. "He's the controller—the mastermind behind this. He plans to use everyone here—as either workers or investors—to build his company." Then she lowered her voice. "I wonder if he is the one who heard us and used one of his thugs to drug us." She touched the back of Michael's neck. "I saw the needle marks there after we found you in the infirmary. They were like the mark some needle made under my arm."

Michael inhaled deeply. "So we'll have to take him out of the picture some way. Once we have him bound, the beings shouldn't be a problem."

"Any ideas? Who knows how many bodyguards are watching him—and us—right now?" Chelsey watched Michael and Neil look at each other for a few seconds then move in opposite directions. She wondered if they carried guns, but now each was too far away for her to ask. She worried that if they rushed Schwatzman, some of his guards would shoot Neil and Michael.

At first, she hadn't noticed how closely the prince had been watching everyone, too. But now she saw he was as aware of everything as she was. Perhaps even more so. For then, Prince Abdul el Fashid made the most unbelievable move. "It is time to act," he whispered and ambled to the side of the pathway that meandered through the center of the city's outskirts. There, he climbed onto and stood upon a large dais that extended from one of the shops. Like a preacher, he inhaled, and first studied the crowd before he raised his arms. "Stop! Everyone," he commanded, as if he were ordering an errant servant. "Stop right now. Everyone on this Heavenly Excursion must listen to me, Prince Abdul el Fashid, immediately. *Your very lives* depend upon hearing my words." He paused.

Suddenly, everything was quiet. Chelsey heard only wind rustling trees and nearby flags. Wondering if everyone would rush the Prince and trample all of them, Chelsey stared at the crowd. She scanned the buildings for an aperture where the prince, Michael, Neil and she could escape—or at least, hide. For a few seconds, everyone stopped moving, as they were in a still frame for a film. In fact, even the slight wind quit blowing. Almost everyone stopped walking toward the city.

But Michael, Neil, Schwatzman, and a few men Chelsey assumed were Schwatzman's bodyguards did not stop. Moving through the crowd like water, they flowed the other direction. Every other person remained motionless, and then, almost in unison, then each turned and looked at the prince.

He spoke slowly. "I am the fifty-sixth prince of the line of the El Fashids," he said, "a family dating back to the 600s." He cleared his throat. But his voice had grown rich, full, and rang of authority. Chelsey had not heard him speak with such confidence and authority before. While she watched him mesmerize the crowd, she grew proud of him.

"However, I am a human being as everyone here is." Turning his palms upward, he raised his arms again and rotated in a semicircle facing the crowd. "And all of us have been duped. Certain greedy men have tried to make fools of us, and they have nearly succeeded." He then crossed his chest and shook his head. "This is no heavenly journey. We are *not* in a heavenly city, but on the outskirts of a city a company built not far from Chungking, China. And that man who built the city has planned to make us slaves in his sweatshops there." With a wide flourish, he raised an arm and pointed at Schwatzman, who now ducked and ran in the direction of the air-ship. "And he plans to take steal body parts from some of us and sell them on the black market." Four men in black followed him. Michael and Neil now chased them.

"Go!" The prince raised his voice until it thundered. He pointed again at Schwatzman. "Stop him and his accomplices—those men in black—before they reach the air ship. Stop them so we can go home."

His words rang through the crowd, which quickly roiled into a mob determined to capture Schwatzman and his crew. A few younger men started after the four bodyguards, and together, Michael and Neil grabbed Schwatzman.

To Chelsey's surprise, Neil held a gun at the CEO's temple. And it was good because Schwatzman's bodyguards were armed. One pulled a gun and aimed it at Neil. Chelsey trembled. Just as the guard was about to shoot Neil, one of the hefty young men jumped on the thug's back and knocked the pistol to the ground. It fired and Chelsey held her breath. The bullet discharged but hit nothing but an outhouse not far from the street.

Schwatzman shook his fist. "You have no proof!" he bellowed.

Unfortunately, there were no local authorities to whom they could take the criminals. Still, men bound the criminals in ropes.

"What will we do with them?" Chelsey asked and looked at the prince. "Even if we return them to the states, Schwatzman's lawyers will get him and these henchmen off."

"Why would I want to return them to the United States?" The prince smiled. "You have forgotten where my realm is located?" He smiled again.

"You would take them back to Lebanon?"

The prince shook his head. He smiled again and his eyes twinkled. "Saudi Arabia."

Chelsey laughed and didn't mind when he embraced her in front of the huge crowd of onlookers. Having appeased any anger by capturing Schwatzman, the crowd applauded. She heard many persons chuckle. Three of the men approached the prince and offered to restrain the criminals. "First, we must find handcuffs to bind these men—or straitjackets, if they are available," the prince said. "Then I will buy everyone food, and we will return to the air-ship. I am certain now I can fly it. Mr. Schwatzman, I am also certain, will happily help instruct me should I have questions. His future: imprisonment, torture, or the death penalty weighs upon his instructions." This time, the prince grinned almost sardonically.

The passage back to Saudi Arabia went much faster, mainly because the airship was not orbiting the earth to make the distance seem farther. The prince claimed that flying the strange-shaped contraption was tantamount to steering other planes. And Chelsey was able to ride in the cabin.

Once they landed, the prince's guard had appeared to lock up Schwatzman, who screamed as an American, he had the right to seek asylum in the Embassy.

"You have forgotten that you have kidnapped a royal prince," Abdul retorted. "And his fiancé."

"You cannot hold me!" Schwatzman railed and once again, shook his fist. "You have no proof!"

"Ahh, but we do," Michael said. "And soon, we'll have far more. International trafficking charges will not allow you asylum in any nation."

Nevertheless, Schwatzman wailed and flailed his arms when three of the prince's guards drug him to an ancient dungeon. "I'll sue!" His voice echoed through the palace halls.

The prince turned to Chelsey. "I was a fool believing it was real."

"He duped many people." She squeezed one of his hands. "And it doesn't mean that the rapture won't happen. This was an artifice of the real thing." She smiled. "Seeing so many who still believe this will happen brings back my faith. This experience has been a gift."

Later, the prince took Chelsey on a tour of the Saudi Arabian palace. Built in the eighth century, its huge domes and geometric designs stretching up the inner walls made it look like a mosque. Gold covered the outside of the main dome, and the rest of the building was so white it glistened. "Tomorrow, you will meet my father, the king."

"I don't know." Chelsey chewed on her lower lip. "I doubt if he will want his son to marry an American. Perhaps I will meet him another time, after we have become better acquainted."

"As you Americans would say—no problem." The prince smiled and drew her hands in his. "One of his wives is an American. She is one of his favorites."

Chelsey shook her head. "You see, that won't work with me. I don't believe in multiple wives. A marriage must stay at a one-to-one ratio." She squeezed his hands. "At least, for me."

The prince drew his eyebrows together and frowned. "Hmmm. I had not truly considered that. It would not be enough to be my favorite wife? You would always be my first wife—the highest status."

She shook her head again. "We must give this much more time. I still have cases to finish in the states. Those cases and the stories I must finish would interfere with our time together." She stared at him, and at once, she began to feel warmth, a faith in something—*perhaps love?*—again. Nevertheless, many items had to be worked out yet. She smiled.

But the prince frowned. "So you are saying we can never be together?" He drew her to the ledge of the balcony that overlooked his estate. "You would give up all of this to write stories? To uncover crime cases?"

"I'm not saying 'never.' I'm saying we must take more time." She smiled again and kissed one of his cheeks. "You have been the one telling me to 'slow down.' Here's my chance to take things slowly."

The prince shrugged. "I was referring to life in general. You will not need those stories as my wife. Running the household and entertaining dignitaries will fill your schedule."

"I'm not ready for that *yet*. Even though I like it here, I couldn't adjust so suddenly." She smiled. "Besides, it isn't like you can't fly across the Atlantic to see me. At least, sometimes."

The prince started to frown but then he looked into her eyes. "Only sometimes? I believe we must make more definite plans than that." Then, he took her hands in his, and together, they turned and looked over the estate below.

www.ingramcontent.com/pod-product-compliance
Lightning Source LLC
Chambersburg PA
CBHW070845250626
47159CB00003B/939